When God Looked Down and Wept

BY

FREDERICK THOMAS GOLDER

BEACHFRONT PRESS

FIRST EDITION, JULY 2015

When God Looked Down and Wept/ Frederick Thomas Golder

ISBN 978-151439646-9

Author photo © 2015 Frederick Thomas Golder

To my wife, Caron and our children

Rachel, David, and Naomi, and to their spouses

Michael, Shera, and Joseph

And to our grandchildren Jared, Noah, Pauline,

Alexandra, Hannah, and Emma

To my mom and dad, Ida and Michael

To my grandparents, Julia and Samuel Golder,

Lena and Jacob Gropman

To the people murdered in the Shoah

and their families

To all the people lost though hatred and ignorance

To a better world

To Judi,

Honored to be invited !

Tikkun Olam !

ACKNOWLEDEGMENTS

My grateful thanks to Shlomo Spak for his many suggestions. Thanks to all those I have met along the way that have encouraged me to write. Special thanks to Peter David Orr for his editing suggestions and help in the design and format of this book.

PROLOGUE

This incredible story is one that was almost not told. More than twelve million people perished in the Holocaust during World War II. Millions of people were imprisoned in Nazi concentration camps; only twenty thousand prisoners survived. Benjamin Sharnofsky was one of the prisoners who barely survived.

I met Benjamin through Leonard Zakim, who was at the time, the New England Regional director for the Anti-Defamation League of B'nai B'rith, an organization founded in 1913 "to stop the defamation of the Jewish people and to secure justice and fair treatment to all." The ADL fights anti-Semitism and all forms of bigotry, defends democratic ideals, and protects civil rights.

I was a member of their Committee, as an attorney, and handled cases of religious discrimination. When Lenny asked me if I would represent Benjamin Sharnofsky in a claim for employment discrimination against the Town of Linwood, initially I refused. I was too busy to take on another pro bono case. Lenny was very persistent. He did not take no for an answer. Lenny finally convinced me that this was a pro bono case that I had to take. When Lenny told me that Benjamin Sharnofsky was terminated because he was "too Jewish," I was hooked. I told Lenny, "In this country, if you want, you can be too Jewish."

I met with Benjamin Sharnofsky to discuss his case for religious discrimination against the Town of Linwood. Benjamin Sharnofsky slowly and painfully related to me the details of his ordeal at the hands of the Nazis. His survival was a miracle; however, I had serious concerns whether he could survive our judicial system.

Eyewitnesses to the Holocaust are dying on a daily basis. Future generations need to learn about these personal accounts to avoid repeating the past.

This book is a true historical account of one man's survival in a time and place where few Jews survived. The facts have been altered to protect the persons involved.

As I listened to Benjamin tell me his story, I could not help thinking about the quote from Martin Niemöller:

"First they came for the Socialists, and I did not speak out--
Because I was not a Socialist.

Then they came for the Trade Unionists, and I did not speak out--
Because I was not a Trade Unionist.

Then they came for the Jews, and I did not speak out-
Because I was not a Jew.

Then they came for me--
and there was no one left to speak for me."

PART ONE

"Any man's death diminishes me, because I am involved in mankind, and therefore never send to know for whom the bells tolls; it tolls for thee."

John Donne

CHAPTER 1

Benjamin Sharnofsky's trial for age and religious discrimination took less than a week. Benjamin knew that his lawyer Sarah Bright did her best, but would that be good enough. Benjamin was sixty-four years old. He had never been in a courtroom before, and now he was sitting in a courtroom waiting for the jury to decide his case, a decision that would have a significant impact on Benjamin and his family. The hardest part of any trial is waiting for the jury to reach a verdict.

The truth is that the parties do not want a fair jury. They want a jury that will favor their side. Each member of the jury comes with his or her biases and prejudices that impact the decision-making process. Benjamin's jury consisted of seven women and five men. Among the jurors, there was one African-American male, a secular Jewish female married to a Christian, and an unemployed male who had recently been laid off. Four of the jurors were under thirty; two were under forty; three were under fifty; and three were under sixty. Only four jurors had college degrees. Five of the seven women were married with children.

"I can't believe I got picked," said the unemployed juror. "How am I gonna get a job stuck here?!"

"What about me?! Who's gonna take care of my kids?" said one of the mothers.

"I don't like it any better than you. I really can't miss time from work," said one of the male jurors.

Initially, each juror was angry about being forced to serve, except for two.

"I know it's hard on all of us, but I think it is our civic duty to serve," said the Jewish juror. Since her married name was Donovan, no one knew she was Jewish, and she had no plans to tell anyone. Every juror with a Jewish sounding name was challenged by the defense and were all excused from serving.

"It's an honor to serve on the jury. It's what makes our country so great," said Frank Scott, the black juror. Except for Donovan, all the other jurors glared at Scott.

1

By the end of the trial, none of the jurors were complaining about serving, at least not openly, to each other.

As Benjamin waited for the jury's verdict, his mind drifted to an earlier time, a time of unimaginable horror, a time of the worst inhumanity, a time when the world stood by and did nothing to stop the madness. Nightmares from that past were always present for Benjamin Sharnofsky, one of a small number of European Jews who survived the Nazi death camps and Hitler's "final solution" for the "Jewish problem" during World War II. It was a miracle that Benjamin survived the Holocaust. Could he survive a trial in an American court?

In 1933, there were over nine million Jews living in Europe. By 1945, close to two out of every three European Jews had been murdered as part of the Nazis' "Final Solution."

Who can explain the inexplicable? Who can make sense out of the senseless? Who can fathom the unfathomable? How could one person be responsible for killing so many? Six million men, women, and children led to the slaughter—for being Jewish. And how could Hitler have had so many willing accomplices?

All the dreams, hopes, and aspirations of millions of people snuffed out. What great inventions and innovations were lost? What great art and ideas that will never be? And what of the offspring of the slaughtered that will never be born? Was the Messiah killed? Were the parents of the Messiah killed? Will there now be no Messiah coming to save us from ourselves? What was lost besides the lives of twelve million innocent people we will never know.

The Germans fell a little short of their goal but still managed to exterminate more than six million Jewish men, women, and children. The Nazi war machine also exterminated more than six million non-Jews, people they considered "undesirable," namely, homosexuals, gypsies, handicapped persons, and others who were not part of the pure Aryan race.

The death toll in World War II was staggering. The estimates range between 60 to 85 million people: 38 to 55 million civilian deaths and 22 to 30 million military deaths.

This was a time that challenged some people's belief in the existence of God; it was a time when even God seemed powerless to stop the insanity.

It was a time "When God looked down and wept."

CHAPTER 2

Benjamin's mind drifted back to the present when he heard the court clerk, "The jury has a question."

The trial judge took his seat and called the lawyers up to the bench.

"The jury has a question. They want to know the difference between the three main branches of Judaism. What do you want me to tell them?" he asked.

Sarah spoke first. "Just explain that there are variations of Judaism as there are of Christianity. While many people classify Judaism into three main branches, Orthodox, Conservative, and Reform, they are not really appropriate. What is important in this case is that Mr. Sharnofsky testified that he is an observant Jew. As an observant Jew, he did not consider that he was part of any particular branch. As an observant Jew, Mr. Sharnofsky believes that Torah, including the Oral Law, was given directly from God to Moses and applies in all times and places. That all Jews are required to live in accordance with the Commandments and Jewish law."

The judge turned to the Linwood School Committee's lawyer, "What do you say to that?"

"I think that you should tell the jury that there are three main branches of Judaism and explain each one," said Ralph Simon, the Linwood School Committee's lawyer.

"With all due respect, your honor, that would not be fair to my client. Jacob Cohen, the chair of the Linwood School Committee, calls himself a Reformed Jew, but he is married to a non-Jew and would not be considered a Jew by anyone that is an observant Jew. The jury would be confused and think, because Mr. Cohen calls himself a Reformed Jew, he is the same as Mr. Sharnofsky. Since Mr. Cohen is a Jew and Mr. Sharnofsky is a Jew, Mr. Cohen would not discriminate against one of his own," Ms. Bright said.

"I think I am going to follow Attorney Simon's suggestion," the judge determined. "I will note your objection Ms. Bright.

You two can write up the three different branches of Judaism, and I will give that to the jury.

"Your honor, Mr. Sharnofsky never testified that he was an Orthodox Jew.   He testified that he is an observant Jew," Ms. Bright implored.

"Ms. Bright, I have made my ruling and have noted your objection.   Mr. Cohen testified that he practiced Reformed Judaism and described the three different branches.   Please prepare the document to submit to the jury," the judge's voice rising in anger.

CHAPTER 3

While the two lawyers worked on the document for submission to the jury, Benjamin's mind drifted back to an earlier time, a happier time remembering his homeland and his family.

On the right bank of the river Tysa at the foothills of the Carpathian Mountains there stretched a picturesque village called Solotvyno. It was there where Benjamin was born on June 27, 1928, to a very religious, observant Jewish family. Benjamin remembered his hometown as "a very lovely and peaceful town." About half the population was Jewish and the other half Romanian. At that time there were close to 10,000 people living in Solotvyno, a small border village that was then part of Czechoslovakia. A small bridge connected Solotvyno to Sighet, a small village in Romania. There were guards or customs inspectors on both sides. The neighboring people living right in the neighborhood of the border did not need any passports. You could cross back and forth freely between the two countries with an Identification Card.

Benjamin's older brother started to study Hebrew at age three. That is the age when all religious Jewish boys started their religious studies. You did not learn much on your third birthday, but you did get sweets and candy to encourage you.

Benjamin remembered one of his earliest memories. "I used to go with him. I was not three yet, and I didn't have to go. I didn't have a teacher, but I went with him on many occasions to hear and to watch the teaching."

Another very early memory was when his father held Benjamin in his hands and taking him across the street to a furrier. Benjamin revered his father. His father had a beard, so his father asked Benjamin if Benjamin wanted a beard and told Benjamin, "The furrier can sew one on."

CHAPTER 4

Solotvyno was a very lively town for its size. There were more businesses and stores than the town really needed. The people from Sighet came to shop in Solotvyno, and the people from Solotvyno went shopping in Sighet, whichever country had the better goods and prices at the time. Czechoslovakia had textiles that were moderately priced, but the textiles in Romania were very expensive.

Before the First World War, there was no Czechoslovakia. The area was originally part of Austria and Hungary, and the national language was Hungarian. They taught Hungarian in the schools. The language spoken in Benjamin's home was Yiddish. Principally the Ashkenazi Jews, who came from eastern and central Europe, used the Yiddish Language. Yiddish, meaning "Jewish," arose between the 9th and 12th centuries in southwestern Germany as an adaptation of Middle High German dialects to the special needs of Jews. To the original German were added those Hebrew words that pertained to Jewish religious life. Later, when the bulk of European Jewry moved eastward into areas occupied predominantly by Slavic-speaking peoples, some Slavic influences were acquired. The vocabulary of the Yiddish spoken in Eastern Europe during recent times comprised about 85% German, 10% Hebrew, and 5% Slavic, with traces of Romanian, French, and other elements. Yiddish is a highly plastic and assimilative language, rich in idioms, and possessing remarkable freshness, pithiness, and pungency. Since it was spoken by ordinary people rather than by scholars, its vocabulary is weak in abstractions. By the same token it has few items descriptive of nature, with which the Jews of Eastern Europe had relatively little contact, and a wealth of words and expressions descriptive of character and of relations among people. It makes liberal use of diminutives and terms of endearment and exhibits a variety of expletives. The use of proverbs and proverbial expressions is considerable. These qualities and usages give Yiddish a uniquely warm and personal flavor. In the early twentieth century an estimated 11 million people living mainly in Eastern Europe and the United States spoke Yiddish. The use of the language has been declining since then. The initial cause was the extermination of the Jewish communities in Poland and other Eastern European countries during World War II. An important factor that also contributed to the decline in usage was the adaptation by Jews to the languages predominant in the United States and in the Soviet Union. In Israel, the Hebrew language is predominant, and Yiddish is a second language, cultivated largely by members of the older generation who have an Eastern European background. In an effort to ensure its preservation, the Hebrew University of Jerusalem teaches Yiddish, as do certain American schools and colleges. Benjamin's father learned the Romanian language from the peasants. His father could not write Romanian, but he could speak it. His father used some Hungarian because he went to a Hungarian school when he was a child in the early part of the century.

When you crossed the bridge from Sighet, you had to climb a hill, a dirt road, and then another one. The second dirt road led to the main street of Solotvyno. There were some businesses there. There was another hill and on top of that hill was a street with the best businesses in the town. Benjamin lived at the bottom of that hill on a corner street.

CHAPTER 5

Benjamin's house was made of thick pieces of wood like railroad ties. The biggest room in Benjamin's house was the store downstairs. Benjamin's family lived above the store and on the side of the store. There were two rooms upstairs; one room was the kitchen and the other was used for sleeping.   Downstairs there were two additional rooms where Benjamin's paternal grandparents lived.

The children slept on the floor in their parents' bedroom and in the kitchen. Benjamin had two older sisters and one older brother. He was the fourth child. He had a brother two years younger and three younger sisters, each born about two years apart.

A family of eight children was not considered unusual. Nobody practiced birth control of any kind. Benjamin's family was affiliated with a Hasidic rabbi. The Jews in Benjamin's town were affiliated with several different Hasidic rabbis. There were dynasties of these Hasidic rabbis. It goes back over two hundred years ago when Hasidic Judaism started in Poland with its founder, Rabbi Bael Shem-Tov. Shem-Tov, meant "the one with the good name."

Hasidic Judaism has several meanings: modest, chaste.   It obtained an additional meaning through usage of a very religious and holy life. Living the life of the Hasidic Judaism is taught to worship God with joy. Hasidic Judaism taught that everybody is equal in God's eyes. Every Jew who serves God is equal to any other.

In Benjamin's hometown of Solotvyno, every Jewish boy received a very strict religious upbringing. Every Hasidic law, every law from the Bible down to the rabbinical literature, whatever was said that you could do or not do, was followed to the letter. The final authority of Jewish behavior was called the Shulchan Aruch. The translation of it meant a ready table, a set table, meaning you have everything there. The Shulchan Aruch is a codification, or written manual, of Jewish law, composed by

Rabbi Yosef Karo in the 16th century. Together with its commentaries, it is considered the most authoritative compilation of Jewish law since the Talmud.[1]

In the Shulchan Aruch you can find all that you would need to live a Jewish life. It deals with how you behave. In the morning when you get up, you have to wash your hands because at night some of the bad spirits may have touched you. So you wash your hands, not with soap and water; that may come later. It is a ritual hand washing. You are not supposed to walk before this ritual hand washing. When you get up, you should have the water right near your bed, and you should not walk with so-called unclean hands. They become unclean while you slept.

There are thousands of these laws in this huge book Shulchan Aruch. How to eat, you have to say the prayer before, and you have to say the prayer after. Regarding food, what is Kosher, what is permitted, what is not permitted. Holidays, what you do, when you do what. You have to have a guide. The Shulchan Aruch is a guide to Jewish religious observations.

All of these laws came, either from the Torah or from later interpretations of the Torah, from the Talmud, and from Maimonides, who himself wrote a book of codes. The ones, which the author of the Shulchan Aruch found most valid, are set forth as a collection of codes of behavior.

That is the way Benjamin and his family lived their lives. From the time they got up until the time they went to sleep at night, they lived God's way. There were three or four different Hasidic rabbis in Solotvyno, and everyone got along very well. Each one went to his or her own temple or shul. There were some families who were not so strict, but Benjamin did not know them or did not know they were not so strict. Benjamin assumed everybody was like his family. Most of the men of the families had beards and long uncut sideburns called *peyes*. They never cut their beards and never trimmed them. Their hair was shaven and on the side they had ear locks. The men who did not look like that offended young Benjamin. He would be insulted and think

---

[1] The Talmud is a record of rabbinic discussions pertaining to Jewish law, ethics, customs, and history. It is a central text of mainstream Judaism.

that he was not a good person. To Benjamin's young mind, a good Jew had to have a beard and peyes.

At age three the custom was that the father would take his boy and wrap him in a prayer shawl and carry him to the Hebrew school on his birthday, and he would get candies there, and the other children would get candies and recite the Hebrew alphabet. This was a tradition that came down from the Middle Ages.

CHAPTER 6

Benjamin's thoughts were again interrupted, this time by his lawyer.

"Benjamin, please look at this paper to make sure it's accurate," as she handed Benjamin the paper that she worked on with Mr. Simon to describe the three branches of Judaism.

Benjamin looked at the document, and said, "How can I comment on this? I only know how I was brought up. I was brought up as an observant Jew. I don't know from Orthodox. I am a Jew who observes traditional Judaism brought to us from the time of Moses. Anyone who does not observe the laws and the Torah is not a Jew. Mr. Cohen married a gentile. He is not a Jew. He calls himself a Reformed Jew. What is that? I know that Mr. Cohen resented me because I practiced real Judaism. I wore a beard with *peyes*. I wore a yarmulke. I observed all the Jewish Holy days. When Mr. Cohen looked at me, he knew he was not a real Jew. Mr. Cohen did not look at me as a regular teacher. I was the Hebrew teacher."

The Linwood School system had a policy that if six or more parents petitioned the high school to have a particular course, the high school had to offer the course. This is how Benjamin Sharnofsky first came to teach at Linwood High School. The parents had petitioned the school to offer classes in Hebrew, and Benjamin was brought in to teach all the Hebrew classes. Benjamin was also certified to teach Spanish and social studies. Since Benjamin had taught in the Linwood School system for more than four years, he was a tenured schoolteacher and could only be removed under very limited circumstances.

As fewer and fewer students opted to study Hebrew as a foreign language, Benjamin saw his classes shrink from five classes to two. In fact Marco Navarro, the head of the Foreign Languages Department actively discouraged students from taking Hebrew classes. There were Spanish classes and social studies classes that were available but rather than assign those classes to Benjamin, Marco Navarro, who was Roman Catholic, assigned two Spanish classes to Mary Frangello, a younger, attractive female teacher and a Roman Catholic, who was not even certified to teach Spanish classes at the time the classes were assigned to her. Mary Frangello was certified to teach Italian at the time and later became certified to teach Spanish. In addition, her evaluations were not as good as Benjamin's evaluations. The head of the Social Studies Department did assign one social studies class for Benjamin to teach, but then for no stated reason, he took away that social studies class the following year and assigned it to a different teacher, who was not even certified to teach social studies.

As class enrollment declined, the Linwood School Committee had to decrease the number of teachers. Benjamin was on the short list. It came down to Benjamin or Mary Frangello.

The principal of the high school, Herb Stein, a secular Jew resented the fact that Benjamin took off every Jewish Holy Day. *Why couldn't Benjamin take off just for Yom Kippur and Rosh Hashanah like all the other Jews?* thought Herb Stein. As far as Stein was concerned, Benjamin took advantage of the Jewish Holidays. In meetings with Jacob Cohen, Stein was concerned about a lawsuit for religious discrimination. Cohen told Stein not to worry, that Cohen knew the people at the Anti-Defamation League[2] and that he would get them to write a letter that there was no religious discrimination if they "laid off" Sharnofsky and retained Mary Frangello.

Benjamin had gone to the Anti-Defamation League for help. They conducted an investigation into Benjamin's claims that he was discriminated against because he was an observant Jew. Unfortunately, Jacob Cohen was able to convince a new intern at the Anti-Defamation League to write a letter stating, "that after a thorough investigation of the Linwood School System, we find that there was no religious discrimination in the case of Benjamin Sharnofsky."

When the chair of the New England Chapter of the Anti-Defamation League found out about this horrible mistake, he was

---

[2] The Anti-Defamation League was founded in 1913 to stop the defamation of the Jewish people and to secure justice and fair treatment for all and serves to fight anti-Semitism and all forms of bigotry.

outraged and fired the intern, but Jacob Cohen released the letter to the press. There was little that could be done, except find the best lawyer they could to represent Benjamin Sharnofsky.

Sarah Bright had one of the best reputations as an advocate for workers and was the Anti-Defamation League's first choice. At first she was very reluctant to take the case, but was finally convinced when she was told that Benjamin lost his job because he was "too Jewish." Sarah told them, "In this country you can be too Jewish. I'll take the case." Sarah agreed to take the case without compensation.

CHAPTER 7

Sarah showed the document to Benjamin. "I agree with you but the judge ordered us to prepare this document to distinguish the three branches of Judaism," she said.

Benjamin looked at the document and said, "It can't be done. The judge doesn't understand."

"We have no choice," she told him. Sarah was having serious doubts about the trial judge being fair and impartial. Before being appointed to the bench, the trial judge served as a mayor of a medium-sized city. It was clear that this trial judge was leaning toward helping the school committee avoid substantial damages. The trial judge had allowed the school committee to introduce the letter from the Anti-Defamation League absolving the school committee of religious discrimination, even though it was hearsay and highly prejudicial. Sarah was justifiably concerned that the jury would place great weight on this letter. If the Anti-Defamation League saw no religious discrimination, why should the jury find any?

"Look Benjamin, I objected to the judge's ruling, but I have no choice but to provide a document for the jury. Let's make it the best one we can," she pleaded.

Benjamin looked at the prepared document. "I don't like it, but if we have to put one in, I guess this is as good as any," Benjamin sighed.

Sarah gave the document to the court clerk. "For the record, do the parties agree that this document may be submitted to the jury?" the clerk asked both attorneys.

"The plaintiff Benjamin Sharnofsky agrees to the submission of this document to the jury subject to our continuing objection," Sarah stated.

"The defendant Linwood School Committee agrees to the submission of this document to the jury without any objection," Attorney Simon reported.

"Since both sides have agreed, I will give this document to the court officer to bring to the jury for their consideration," the court clerk declared as he handed the document to the court officer. The clerk continued, "Since it is almost one o'clock, the judge has told me to inform you that we will take our lunch recess now. Please report back at two o'clock. This court will stand in recess until two o'clock.

The parties left the courtroom and, except for Benjamin, they all went to lunch. Benjamin brought his own lunch, an apple. He did not eat food that was not kosher. He sat outside the courtroom eating his apple, deep in his own thoughts of a much happier time.

When Benjamin's father brought him to Hebrew school, Benjamin felt great. It meant that you mattered. You went two or three times a week to pick up a few more letters and then put together the letters and start reading syllables.

By the age of five, Benjamin could read Hebrew. He could read the prayers. He did not know what they meant, but he could read them. When Benjamin turned five, he began going to Hadar. In Hebrew this means a room. But for Benjamin, it was *the* room. Hadar meant a specific room where a rabbi was teaching children.

When Benjamin turned five, he went to Hadar every day for two to three hours where he learned to daven. The rebbe taught *Humash*, the five books of Moses. Davening, that means to pray. Nobody knows its origin.

When Benjamin turned six, he went to first grade in a Czech public school because his town was part of Czechoslovakia at the time. There was no kindergarten or pre-kindergarten. Benjamin went to public school five days a week starting at 8:00 o'clock sharp. The end of the day varied between 11:30 a.m. and 12:30 p.m. There was about a half-hour for lunch or to play a little. The rabbi knew what time the students got out. If they got out early, sometimes the boys would lie to him so they could play a little soccer outside of the school. A few of the boys would get together to make sure nobody went early. If one of them went early, they would all get in trouble. Most of the people Benjamin went to school with were Jewish. There may have been one or two Hungarians, but mostly Jewish. The Romanians had their own school.

Although there were no Czechs where Benjamin lived, his town became part of Czechoslovakia overnight, and the public school taught the Czech language, its history, and its government.

This was all taught in the Czechoslovakian language. They paid Czech taxes. They had Czech passports, and Czech people conducted all official businesses. Even though no one was Czechoslovakian, everything in school was in Czech. They imported teachers from the motherland, and they even built apartments for the teachers. So for the first time Benjamin had to learn Czech. Benjamin did not understand a thing in the beginning. After a while, Benjamin caught on. By the second grade, Benjamin could answer questions in Czech to the teacher. By the fourth and fifth grades, Benjamin was fluent in Czech. His parents learned Czech from Benjamin. They wrote little notes if they had to deal with certain business, but Benjamin's father conducted his business mostly in German. This was the commercial language in Europe at that time.

In the middle of the fourth grade, Benjamin and his family became Ukrainians overnight. This was a political act engineered by Hitler. Teachers were brought in to teach the Ukrainian language. The Czechs were out and the Ukrainians were in. The teachers, who did not know a word of Czech, were teaching children who did not understand this new language. Benjamin did not understand a word. The Ukrainians were there for about four months, and then war broke out. Hitler attacked Russia, took the land back, and gave it to Hungary, his ally. That is how Benjamin became Hungarian.

Benjamin's family was originally part of the Austrian/Hungarian Empire before the war. Benjamin's parents spoke Hungarian because it was Hungary before the First World War. There were even some children who spoke it. Benjamin did not, but Hungary was not a completely strange language in the town that used to be part of Hungary.

Hungary is a very difficult language. Benjamin started learning Hungarian. The first few months Benjamin understood nothing, but he never failed a test. The teachers allowed for the fact that the students did not know the language, that they could not take a test properly or even answer questions, not because they did not know the answer, but because they could not say it. Benjamin went to public school until the age of twelve.

As soon as he finished public school for the day, he went to Hebrew school.

CHAPTER 8

The people in Benjamin's neighborhood had a very happy childhood within their own families. The whole family as a unit was your first unit, and then the place where you prayed, the rabbi of the town was your second family.

Benjamin would go to religious service twice each day, once in the morning and then in the afternoon. When he was four, he started going every day. The children had their service in Hadar when their parents davened in the shul (synagogue). This is how the children learned the prayer book. There were about 16 or 18 students around a table, and you read a segment and when you made mistakes, the teacher would correct you.

On the Sabbath the children did not go until the afternoon. On the Sabbath they would go for a couple of hours in the afternoon and the instruction was different. The rabbi could do whatever he wanted. He could tell stories if he wanted to, and some were great storytellers. They jolted your imagination. All of this was spoken in Yiddish.

These rituals only applied to Benjamin and his brothers. Girls were not required to have a strict Jewish education. Each girl learned from her mother how to be a Jewish woman, how to keep Kosher. They learned that from their mothers, and girls were also given reading lessons in Hebrew, but that was all.

There was a central synagogue to which everybody belonged, whether you went there or not. Most heads of households bought a seat there before the synagogue was built. Benjamin's town had a synagogue, a large building, and it also had a smaller synagogue, not a chapel, as it is called today, but it served as a chapel in the smaller synagogue where people started going weekdays. In the smaller synagogue you went at 5:00 o'clock in the morning. There you would find some people, 10 or 20. In the evening, late at night, after the services, there was a whole library in the synagogue, usually filled with elderly people who loved to study. It was their entertainment, their enjoyment, and their joy to feel close to it. The people were very close to the Talmud, and all the subsequent religious texts.

There were few radios in the town. Benjamin's family could barely afford necessities. Benjamin had no need for a radio and did not miss it.

"Come on Benjamin, let's go back into Court," Sarah said jolting Benjamin back to the present.

"How long do we have to wait?" Benjamin asked.

"There really is no way of knowing," Sarah replied.

"Is this good or bad for our case?" Benjamin asked.

"There's no way of telling," Sarah replied.

"So we just wait?" Benjamin asked.

"That's all we can do and hope for the best," Sarah said.

All we can do is pray, thought Benjamin.

Once again Benjamin's mind drifted back to the past. Benjamin's father owned a general village store that sold mainly groceries, but also had all kinds of other merchandise including clothing, porcelain, china, and glasses. A general store that had everything.

When Benjamin's sisters were older, they worked in the store. Benjamin was too young to sell. Customers would not want a child to serve them.

Benjamin's father had a seat in the central synagogue. Not everybody did, but everybody who was somebody did buy a seat prior to the building of the synagogue. Benjamin's family did not always go to that synagogue. Weekdays, they would go to the smaller synagogue that was part of the main synagogue. Saturday is the holiest day in Judaism. Saturday was the height of uplifting, an emotional high. You could sense it already on Friday afternoons when everybody went to the mikvah.

The mikvah was the public bath. There was no running water at that time. Friday you went to the mikvah to wash. The mikvah was like a small Jacuzzi without the bubbles. The mikvah has warm water in it, and you have to dip yourself in the mikvah several times before every holiday. It is a ritual bath, a spiritual cleansing. There were people who went to the mikvah early in the morning on weekdays. The men would all bathe naked in the mikvah on designated weekdays. The women would also go separately into the mikvah for a ritual bathing. The mikvah was small, maybe 6 feet by 10 feet. The mikvah was in a separate building. It had nothing to do with the synagogue.

The organized Jewish community collected taxes for religious purposes that were separate from the collection of taxes by the town. The Jewish tax was mostly paid through the butcher by having a tax on the price of meat. If meat cost a dollar a pound, they charged $1.50 and $.50 was like a tax that was paid to the religious leaders for their services to the community.

There were three main religious appointed positions in the town: the rabbi, the shochet, and one trained rabbi called the Dayan, the judge. These were all religious appointments. They were all highly educated people.

The shochet was the one who slaughtered the animals. The animal had to be killed with respect and compassion by a shochet (ritual slaughterer), a pious Jew who has in mind the life of the animal as he drew the knife across its neck.

The Dayan was the judge of matters of Jewish religion. If you had a question, you are in doubt about something or you drop milk into the meat, something went awry and you did not know what the situation was – were the dishes still okay or do you throw them out – you went to the rabbi. If he was not around, you went to the Dayan. And those two people answered religious questions about food. There were other problems too; two partners in a business had a problem, they went to the Dayan.

The leaders have to be elected by the people in the Jewish community. If there was a change, there had to be an election. But throughout Benjamin's childhood, the same family dominated the town leadership, the Slomovich family. Although the head of the town was like a president, he was not called a president. He was called head of the community, Rosh Hakoho.

CHAPTER 9

The services on Saturday were a religious high. To young Benjamin seeing all these people, young and old, davening feverishly before the venerable rabbi was indescribable.

The ritual baths were taken on Friday afternoon, and then Benjamin would come home with his father and change into clean clothes. Children did not wear underwear, but they had two suits, one for weekdays and one for the Sabbath. When the one you used on the weekdays wore out, your Sabbath suit would become your weekday suit, and your parents would buy you a new suit for the Sabbath. This would usually happen on Passover. Passover was the time you usually received new things, if you could afford them.

Friday evenings were when the angels came to your house. Benjamin's father was very religious, and he sang Shalom Aleichem with his children. Shalom Aleichem is a traditional song sung Friday night at the beginning of the Jewish Sabbath, welcoming the angels who accompany a person home on the eve of the Sabbath. Benjamin knew the translation of the words, but he was taught them in another context. They were welcoming the angels of peace to his home. Benjamin could feel their presence.

Benjamin's father would then say Kiddush. *Kiddush* is a blessing recited over wine or grape juice to sanctify the Sabbath. The Torah refers to two requirements concerning Shabbat - to "keep it" and to "remember it." Jewish law therefore requires that Shabbat be observed in two respects. One must "keep it" by refraining from thirty-nine forbidden activities, and one must "remember it" by making special arrangements for the day, and specifically through the Kiddush ceremony.

Kiddush is sanctification of the day, sanctification through prayers that you are chanting; and the kiddush is the symbol of the holiday, the wine, the goblet of wine, usually not a glass, but a nice goblet, silver or otherwise, usually a silver goblet.

The Friday dinner was usually the same. If fish could be bought, they had a little fish. It was not available all the time, or it was too expensive. They had chicken soup with noodles but no matzo balls in Benjamin's hometown. If there was no fish, they would have a piece of boiled chicken and challah, a special braided bread eaten on the Sabbath and Jewish holidays. Benjamin's family ate very little meat.

Benjamin's family was poor. Benjamin's father may have been not as poor in Benjamin's early childhood years. The store was doing pretty well until the Hungarians came in 1939 and took away his father's license. Hungary had its own anti-Semitic laws just like Germany.

Germany passed the Nuremberg Laws in 1935 that deprived Jews of citizenship and prohibited marriage between Jews and other Germans. The laws classified people as German if all four of their grandparents were of "German or kindred blood," while people were classified as Jews if they descended from three or four Jewish grandparents. A person with one or two Jewish grandparents was a crossbreed, of mixed blood. The Nuremberg Laws reduced the Jews to nothing. They could not own anything. They were fired from their jobs. Hungary had similar laws, not as severe as the Germans, but Hungary was allied with Germany.

CHAPTER 10

Benjamin did not understand the significance of the Nazis running Hungary. He only knew that Jews were not allowed to have certain businesses. There were ten grocery stores in Benjamin's town. Eight were closed down; two were left open. Benjamin did know why. Why were two left open? By lot? By bribes? He never found out.

Overnight, Benjamin's father lost his livelihood. As meager as it was, he lost it all in one day in 1940. Benjamin was already 12 years old. Benjamin was devastated, but he kept it inside. After all, it was accepted that if you were a Jew you suffered. Jews who did not live in Palestine were in exile. All Jews who lived throughout the world were in exile. Jews were persecuted, and their persecution was nothing new. It went on for centuries.

Benjamin had very little to eat. Benjamin's father used to have another income in addition to his store. Benjamin's father was matched through a matchmaker with Benjamin's mother, who came from a small village about 10 or 15 kilometers away on the Romanian side. Benjamin's mother came from a wealthy family. Benjamin's maternal grandfather owned acres of land and had a small oil factory. He made oil from sunflower seeds. As a dowry for his wedding, he gave Benjamin's father half an apple orchard not far from his village where he planted apple trees. In a good season, there was quite a bit of money in selling the apples and shipping them off to Prague, Czechoslovakia where the price of apples was high. Perhaps his father could make an extra $2,000.00. In a bad season his father would earn very little money. It all depended on the weather. After Benjamin's father lost his store, he could no longer pay his debtors.

Benjamin's paternal grandfather was a shoemaker. Benjamin's father was not, but he learned some of this trade while he was a child watching his father. Benjamin's father had the tools that his father left for him, so Benjamin's father started fixing shoes to make a few pennies. Benjamin felt awful because Benjamin's father was a scholar, well respected in the community, especially in the rabbi's synagogue, but also in the town, even though his family was poor. The town did not only honor people who were rich but honored people for other reasons. Benjamin's father was known in the town because he was born there. His family had lived in the town for several generations. He owned a house in town. He had a store. Benjamin felt that his father was humiliated by losing his store. He was not really a shoemaker, but he was trying to make money anyway he could to support his family. Benjamin felt humiliated for his father and for himself. But these were bad times. There was a war. They lived in a country where Jews were persecuted. As a Jew, you accepted this and hoped it would not last very long. Whenever there was a war going on, eventually it had to end. And Benjamin knew this war would end soon. It would not be a 30-year war or a 100-year war. This would be like the First World War, four or five years, and Benjamin's family knew Germany was losing.

They knew this after Stalingrad. When Russia attacked, the Germans fled. Some went through Benjamin's town in the summer of 1941. Benjamin was then thirteen.

CHAPTER 11

When Benjamin was twelve, he left Solotvyno and went to Sighet to study at the Yeshiva level. Yeshiva was for older boys, teen-agers. Very few Jewish boys studied at the Yeshiva level. A father who studied the Talmud wanted his boys to study the Talmud at the Yeshiva. Talmud is very serious, and the need to know the Talmud is taken very seriously. Talmud is a compilation and the discussion of laws as expressed by early Jewish scholars in the second and third century. It contains laws. It contains arguments for the law or arguments against a particular law.

The Talmud consists of interpretations of the Jewish laws. It has personal stories. It is a whole encyclopedia consisting of about thirty-six huge volumes. It contains commentaries about difficult passages. It is written mostly in Aramaic. One volume is in Babylonian.

The method for studying the Talmud is to read each line with the teacher translating every word for the student in Yiddish. The students also learn the Aramaic language as each line is read. The method is all done orally, nothing is written down.

Benjamin's older brother, Simcha, was a sickly child, and he did not start school when he was six. He started school when Benjamin did. Even though Simcha was older, they were in the same grade. When Benjamin was twelve, Benjamin's father asked Benjamin if he wanted to go to study in Sighet. It took thirty minutes walking from one center of the town to the other. Crossing the bridge took less than two minutes. There is no bridge there today. Benjamin wanted to go for two reasons: Every child wants to be away from home, and also because Benjamin wanted to be in the environment of the rabbi in Sighet, which was a much larger town.

Benjamin's father rented a room for Benjamin -- for two. A friend of Benjamin's father also sent his son to Sighet. The two roomed in a house not far from the Yeshiva.

Benjamin's best friend was David Pearl. He was Benjamin's age. They went to public school together. And they spent hours after school together. Benjamin loved David, and David loved Benjamin.

For the first time Benjamin's father gave Benjamin a choice. Everything up to that point he ordered. He was a very strict father; he decided everything. He never asked -- never. Benjamin was so surprised that his father gave him the choice. He asked and Benjamin said, "I want to go to Sighet." So that was it. Benjamin went to Sighet.

Benjamin went to Sighet but it only lasted for about a half a year. It dissolved because of economic reasons. While Benjamin was in Sighet, he came home once in a while but did not like to come home. Benjamin wanted to be next to the rabbi and all the singing. Benjamin was part of the choir there. Every day of the week Benjamin ate at a different house. The Yeshiva did not have any kitchen. Benjamin's father who knew many people in Sighet and had distant relatives in Sighet went to his relatives and said, "Would you accept my son to give him a day's food once a week?" This was a traditional way of subsidizing Jewish education.

It was a mitzvah[3] to provide for a student who studied Torah. Since the Middle Ages, this was a prevalent custom for Jewish households to provide food and education by having a boy come once a week to your house to be fed. One family could have three or four boys in a week and have someone every day, if they could afford it.

These families would feed you breakfast, lunch and dinner. One day a week you would go to somebody's house for breakfast, lunch and dinner. Benjamin went to seven different families. Benjamin went once a week to the richest man in town, a distant relative of Benjamin's father. The man's son later became head of the *Shin Bet*.[4]

His son survived. Benjamin knew him at home when he ate at his parents' table. His name was Simon, Simon Mendelovich. He was a boy of sixteen or seventeen at the time. He had a younger brother, who was about the same age as Benjamin. He did not survive.

---

[3] A good deed.
[4] The Israel Security Agency.

The meals depended on the economic condition of the family. Some families fed you better; some gave you whatever they had.

Benjamin became bar mitzvahed while in Sighet. At that time Benjamin's father was so poor, so destitute, that for Benjamin's bar mitzvah, he did not invite Benjamin back home to celebrate Benjamin's bar mitzvah in the house, the Kiddush. The Kiddush is the food served after a bar mitzvah celebration. Benjamin's parents could not afford to have Benjamin's bar mitzvah, so Benjamin stayed in Sighet. But during the week, his father brought a bottle of some drink and some cookies and cake and gave it to an older Yeshiva man there to have it for Sabbath when Benjamin would be called to the Torah. This was Benjamin's bar mitzvah to have the Kiddush, cookies, and drink. During the service, Benjamin did the Maftir. The Maftir is the last person called to the Torah reading and the Haftorah -- the chanting. A chapter from the prophets, it is chanted, by the Bar Mitzvah boy.

The Haftorah reading is a chapter from the prophets. This is already preassigned. Every week there is a different portion from the prophets at the conclusion of the Torah reading. During the service, it was Benjamin's bar mitzvah, and they did not believe him. They thought he was joking to get the Maftir. One of them said, "Yes, his father left the Kiddush and today is his bar mitzvah." No one at Benjamin's family was present at Benjamin's bar mitzvah.

The students had a separate service davening. They did not daven with the adults. Benjamin's father could have come, but it would have been out of place. No adult or married man went, only Yeshiva boys. There were forty or fifty students in the Yeshiva. Benjamin's father did the minimum, and it was the most he could do. Benjamin did not blame his father. Benjamin understood. Benjamin's had his bar mitzvah without his father, mother, brothers, and sisters who were less than two miles away. Benjamin did not feel slighted because he knew that his father and mother loved him. Benjamin's father came to see him whenever he could and would bring Benjamin something.

CHAPTER 12

One time Benjamin's father came to see Benjamin on a Friday afternoon, and Benjamin was in the community bath. Benjamin was in the steam room and somebody called out, "Your father is here." Since he did not find Benjamin in his room or in the synagogue, he found Benjamin there.

Benjamin's mother was two years younger than his father. She was born in 1896 and was 22 or 23 when she married Benjamin's father. Benjamin's mother came from a small village. She knew the village language of Romanians in that neighborhood. She spoke their kind of Romanian because the Romanian language is not the same in every area. Benjamin's mother had a Jewish education. Her father was also a great scholar, and her father gave Benjamin's father a dowry, not only half of an apple orchard but also a thirty–six volume, leather bound set of the *Vilner Talmud*. Benjamin's father used it frequently.

Benjamin's mother was very religious and did not get along with Benjamin's father's brother, her brother-in-law. Benjamin left his parents at an age when he did not know them yet. He only knew them as father and mother. He did not know much about them as people and that hurt Benjamin a great deal because there were thousands of questions he would have liked to have asked them about their childhood, about the family, and he never had the chance.

Benjamin's mother would take Benjamin to her town when she went to visit her father. He was by then a very old man. She was the youngest in her family. She would take Benjamin because if she did not Benjamin would cry.

When she went to visit her father, she would usually take only one of her children. Benjamin's mother had a very hard life just as every mother did in those days.

There was no running water in the house. Across the street there was a public faucet from a reservoir. You could take as much water as you wanted. Anybody could go there with a pail, fill it up, and take the water into the house. Some people had to walk a longer distance to get the water. You bathed indoors. There was an outhouse behind the house. Every house had an outhouse. There were no machines for laundry. There was no gas for cooking, no electricity. You cooked on a wooden stove. The top was heated with wood and even the oven where you baked was heated with wood. Benjamin's mother had to heat water, carry water from outside to the house, heat the water, and do the dishes at home. During the summer when it was warm, sometimes they would go to the river to wash the linen.

All the food was organic and everything was natural. Food was kept in the cellar. There were no refrigerators. The cellar walls were made of bricks. Benjamin's father also used the cellar to store potatoes. He would buy a wagon or two of potatoes, and sell the potatoes, especially before Passover. People would buy a lot of potatoes on Passover because you could not eat bread. Benjamin's father was a very honest man. There were business people who would cheat on the weight, but not Benjamin's father.

CHAPTER 13

Benjamin had a good voice as a child, an alto. So he would be one of the three or four boys who made up the choir at the rabbi's *tish.*[5] What was conducting a *tish*? Friday night after the services, everybody went home to their families to have the Sabbath meal. Afterwards, many fathers and their sons went back to the rabbi. The rabbi had a big room with a huge, long, square table like a conference room with benches on each side and his special chair was at the head of the table. The rabbi was from Sighet, a beautiful and kind man, younger than Benjamin's father. He was in his thirties when Benjamin knew him. His father died young. His father, a renowned Hasidic rabbi, died young, in his mid 20's, of a heart attack. His oldest son was only 17 and he took over his father's position. He was the official rabbi of Sighet. He was paid a salary by the town.

On Friday night, a couple of hours after service, they would go to the rabbi's house and come to his table. They came to participate in his meal service. The rabbi had a *Gabai*. A *Gabai* was his assistant or sort of a secretary and manager. He was always with him. He always escorted him everywhere he went. Benjamin knew the *Gabai* very well. The *Gabai* had several children, and Benjamin knew them. The *Gabai* was a great scholar and a sweet man. He was about 50 years old. The rabbi would come on Friday evening for the *tish* with his *Gabai*. The *Gabai* would stand right behind him. A few boys were chosen as helpers of the *Gabai* with the singing. There is much singing going on. Benjamin was one of the boys singing. Benjamin's voice could be distinguished because it was an alto, and it was very clear. The rabbi immediately realized that and asked Benjamin to be part of the choir. The rabbi would stand up and the yeshiva boys would sing the Shalom Aleichem and would say the prayer and everybody would sit down afterward, and the rabbi would be served his meal. They would bring him one plate at a time. He

---

[5] Table.

would not eat all of it. He would get a portion too large for him. He would eat a little of it, and the rest would be divided. Everybody got a little piece. This was very important, to eat the leftovers of the rabbi. He deliberately had a large portion, ate a little bit, and then it was passed around. It is called *shirayim.*[6] This is supposed to be good for you, that you have eaten the same food with this godly man, and there is singing. and then the rabbi says his *drosho.*[7] He would start something and develop a topic, build upon it. It was like a symphony.

The Sighet yeshiva was very small. The Town of Sighet was itself a very small town, and in the bad economic times, Sighet could not support a large yeshiva. Benjamin studied in Sighet and was bar mitzvahed there. He studied in the Sighet yeshiva from the spring of 1941 to early fall when it dissolved. It dissolved because the town could no longer afford to subsidize it.

Benjamin lived there even though he was only a half an hour away from home. Benjamin and another boy rented a room with a family, but they had nothing to do with the family. They did not eat there. They did not have to go through their house because there was a side door.

Benjamin was 12 years old at the time. A typical day was simply the regular typical day for every yeshiva bocher (student), for every religious Jew. You got up in the morning and went to prayers. You had a minyan. A minyan is a quorum of ten adult males. Ten adults can have a minyan, a service. You go to your prayers.

There are some different explanations for the minyan. One of them goes back to the time when Abraham was asking God to save Sodom and Gomorrah, and he asked God, "Why would you destroy the city? What if I find 50 good people in there?" God said, "Okay, you find me 50 good people, I'll let them go. It went down to 30, then to 20, and God still said yes, and it went down to 10, and God still said, "Yes, I will abstain from destroying them if you find me ten good people." Ten was the last number, and Abraham could not find even ten good men. He could not find a minyan, not even that. That is why the cities were destroyed.

---

[6] Leftovers from the rabbi.
[7] A Torah talk, a sermon.

That is one of the explanations for a minyan of ten. There may be other explanations.

When the Sighet yeshiva broke up, Benjamin went home like everybody else. In September after the high holidays, both Benjamin's older brother Simcah and Benjamin went to a yeshiva in Hungary. They went to Nyiregyhaza because they had a few cousins there. Benjamin's father wrote to one of them and asked to see if he could set them up to have a place to sleep when they arrived. There were two yeshivas in Nyiregyhaza. Benjamin's brother went to one, and Benjamin went to the other one. Benjamin's brother was a house *bocher* (student, assistant). He was always there with the rabbi.

Benjamin's brother studied with this revered scholar, the Vitker Rabbi, who was very well known in Hungary. Benjamin did not go with his brother because that rabbi did not conduct a regular yeshiva. He taught a few boys, but he did not have a regular yeshiva class.

CHAPTER 14

In the summer of 1942, Benjamin's brother got into some trouble. In those days food was rationed. In Hungary proper where they were, there was rationing. There was enough food because Hungary was very rich in agriculture and wheat and corn, but Solotvyno, where Benjamin came from, there was a famine, so Benjamin's brother sent home bread by mail because he could buy bread. Then he got an idea to send home some bread coupons within the bread. He cut open the bread and put some coupons in so Benjamin's father could redeem them at home. Benjamin's brother got caught buying these coupons from somebody. He got caught with the man who sold them. They were both taken to the police station, and they were beaten up brutally. The adult was a man of about thirty.

What Benjamin's brother did was an illegal act, just like you would sell food stamps. You are not supposed to sell them for liquor or cigarettes. You are supposed to use them for bread. Now, he had these coupons, which was illegal. They were not his coupons. He bought coupons. There was a market in it, all over the country. After they beat him up, they released him. He was afraid to stay in this town any more. He decided to leave. He was afraid they would call him in again. They were still investigating. Since it was just before Rosh Hashanah, before the New Year, Benjamin and his brother decided to go to Ratzferd, a town not far from Nyiregyhaza.

There was a very important Hasidic rabbi of a great dynasty in Ratzferd. His name was Sholemeliezer, a son-in-law of the Sance Rabbi, a famous Hasidic rabbi in Poland. They went there for Rosh Hashanah. They could not afford to rent a room, so they slept on an upholstered, old chair in the synagogue. Since they did not want to go home, they went by foot to Debrecen, the second largest city in Hungary. They walked because they were afraid to go on the train.

It was a long walk, but they also hitchhiked. Some peasants took them up on top of their hay wagon. They got a ride to another town. That night was the night before Yom Kippur. The next morning was Erev Yom Kippur, and they found a family to take them in to sleep. In the very early morning they went to the Slichot service.

Slichot are special prayers said before Rosh Hashanah until Yom Kippur. It starts the Sunday before Rosh Hashanah. If Rosh Hashanah falls on a Monday, it starts the Sunday before that. Usually the Sunday before Rosh Hashanah all the way through Yom Kippur there is a special service in addition to the morning prayers. There are special prayers for that period which is the period, the Days of Awe. The whole month of awe has special prayers. They got up with this family, with this man about four o'clock in the morning to go to Slichot service. The town of Hajdunans was filled with soldiers. When they got out of the services, they were afraid because at that time if soldiers saw boys with the payes, they usually beat them up for the fun of it. Fortunately, nothing happened, and they made it back to the home with this man, and then they hitchhiked all the way to Debrecen. In Debrecen they had a cousin, a sister of the cousins from Nyiregyhaza.

They stayed there for Yom Kippur, and Benjamin had the pleasure of going to the school in Debrecen that had a very famous cantor by the name of Silver. After Yom Kippur, Benjamin's brother had been told about a yeshiva in upper Hungary, and he went his own way and left Benjamin in Debrecen. Benjamin then went to visit his uncle and aunt, the parents of these cousins, who lived not far from Nyiregyhaza in a city called Kalev. This was the Yiddish name of the town. The Hungarian name was called Nagykallo. The aunt was Benjamin's mother's only sister. Her name was Rivka. Benjamin's uncle's name was Yitzchak.

It was Sukkot. It was in Kalev, in this town that Benjamin heard about a yeshiva in Bekescsaba. That is where Benjamin went next. Benjamin was now alone in Bekescsaba in the fall of 1942. Benjamin was in Bekescsaba for two and a half years, up to the German occupation.

CHAPTER 15

Bekescsaba was a fairly good size town with a small yeshiva. You established yourself there by going to the rabbi, telling him where you were from, telling him where you studied, and telling him your troubles. If he liked you, he would take care of you. Benjamin's parents send him a small sum of money to pay for the room. Benjamin's parents were in extreme poverty at that time.

Benjamin was thirteen and a half and was on his own. He appeared before the rabbi, a tall, fat man, great scholar, very friendly man, liked life, and he interviewed Benjamin. He said, "Okay, I'll keep you, I'll take you." He sent Benjamin to a Balebos.

Everybody that owns a house is a Balebos. It comes from Hebrew, but it is corrupted from the original Hebrew into Yiddish. You are the Balebos at your house, and you are the Balebos at an office. They called the hosts that were going to give food for the day the Balebos. Head of the household is a good translation. The rabbi sent Benjamin to several heads of households to ask to be given a day of food for that day of the week. The rabbi had a list of families who would give food to Yeshiva boys. The rabbi sent Benjamin to a few households. Soon Benjamin had every day of the week lined up. Every day of the week Benjamin had a place to go and have three meals, breakfast early in the morning, lunch, and then dinner in the evening.

The rabbi liked Benjamin. Benjamin was the youngest person at the Yeshiva, and Benjamin was singing beautifully, and he knew beautiful melodies, Hassidic nigunim.[8] The Rabbi liked Benjamin to sing for him at the table. On Shabbat you are supposed to have

---

[8] A form of Jewish religious songs or tunes sung by a group. Nigunim are especially central to worship in Hasidic Judaism, which evolved its own structured, soulful forms to reflect the mystical joy of intense prayer.

three meals, Friday night, Saturday lunchtime, and Saturday late afternoon before it gets dark, just as the Shabbat ends.

It is customary for most rabbis, even non-Hasidic rabbis to have guests at his table. They do not come to eat. They just come to keep him company. It is called *gehen zum tisch*, to go to the table. After eating at home, you would sometimes go to the table of your own rabbi. This is a Hasidic custom that the rabbi does not eat alone on holidays, not only Shabbat but other holidays too. He eats in a room with a large table, and the people come before he even enters. When he enters, everybody stands up in respect. People sit around a long table, the Rabbi, of course, sits at the head of the table, and the boys do not take seats, only the old men take seats, and then the rabbi comes in. His assistant tells him the house is full and then he comes in. This happened in Sighet, and it happened in Solotvyno also. They would go to Solotvyno to the rabbi's *tisch*.

This rabbi of Bekescsaba was a Misnagid, an opponent of the Hasidic sects. He was just as religious and just as studied and just as observant, except he did not accept the authority of the rabbi. There was nothing against the Hasidic rabbis, but this rabbi was not a Hassidic rabbi, so you did not go to *zum tisch*. Instead, late Saturday afternoon you went to Mincha service.[9] Mincha service was every day. You talked about the Shabbat service, which is a little more than every day because you read from the Torah, and you called three people to the Torah, and you would daven.[10] You daven at the Mincha service.

After Mincha comes the *shalash sudis* (third meal), when you sit down at a table, and everybody gets a roll in order to say the prayer before, and then say the grace after meal. *Shalash sudis* is a symbolic meal, a very light meal, but *shalash sudis* can take a good hour because there is a lot of singing going on of poems written hundreds of years ago. These poems are called Zmiros. Zmiros

---

[9] The shortest prayer service of the day takes place in the afternoon, or at least just before sunset, and is called Mincha. It is composed of the recitation of Psalm 145, the Amidah, a prayer of repentance and the concluding prayer to all Jewish prayer services, Aleynu. Aleynu is a reaffirmation of Jewish goals and a hope for the better world for all humankind.

[10] To pray.

are poems written in the middle ages. The topic is always the holy and restful day of Shabbat. Some of them are so beautiful that they are included in the prayer book, and they are designated for Shabbat singing, either Friday night at a Shabbat meal or Shabbat morning or at *shalash sudis*. At *shalash sudis* Benjamin was the star. The rabbi liked Benjamin's voice. Benjamin had a very good alto voice and could sing a good *nigun*.[11]

---

[11] A Chassidic melody.

CHAPTER 16

Benjamin came from Solotvyno and Sighet and was soaked in that tradition there. Benjamin knew some beautiful *nigunim*.[12] The rabbi would say in his deep voice, "Binyomin, sog this piece and then another." Benjamin's Hebrew name is Binyomin. "Sog" means sing in Yiddish. After a while, the whole table sang along. Benjamin was the star there. When Benjamin sang at the rabbi's table, people outside would listen. The neighbors stood around the house listening. Once or twice it happened some balebos[13] told the rabbi, "Give me Benjamin for a Shabbat." That was very uplifting for a young kid, for his self-esteem.

A typical day at the yeshiva was getting up early for the service or even earlier to study first and then have the morning service, then study the rest of the day, except for a break for lunch.

Benjamin would study the lesson of the week, usually Talmud. The Talmud is not strictly law. The Talmud is treating, discussing and arguing over many different subjects. In Bekescsaba in addition to Talmud, there was the *Yoreh De'ah*.[14] You studied until the evening service, then you had dinner, and then you studied again until you went to sleep. You studied all day. The younger boys received help from the older ones. Sometimes an older boy, eighteen or nineteen, was assigned to help you. Sometimes you just went and asked anybody.

---

[12] Nigunim are largely improvisations, though they could be based on thematic passage and are stylized in form, reflecting the teachings and charisma of the spiritual leadership of the congregation or its religious movement. Nigunim are especially central to worship in Hasidic Judaism, which evolved its own structured, soulful forms to reflect the mystical joy of intense prayer.

[13] A Jewish master of the house: a Jewish house owner or host.

[14] Yoreh De'ah is a code of law written in Hebrew.

The Talmud is not written in Hebrew. The Talmud is written in Aramaic. There are no punctuation marks or vowels. There is no separation of phrase or sentence. It is all just ongoing words. It is difficult in the beginning, but once you know it you do not need all of those helpers like vowels and punctuation marks.

Benjamin went home for Passover for two weeks. Benjamin was only three or four hundred kilometers from home. Benjamin came home by train. Benjamin had to change trains several times. The last train took Benjamin into Sighet right next to the bridge. Benjamin went home alone. Then after the holidays when Benjamin went back, he took his younger brother with him. His brother had just been Bar Mitzvahed. His name was Chayim Hersh. Benjamin took care of him because in Bekescsaba Benjamin was already well established. Everybody knew Benjamin. The rabbi liked him, not only for Benjamin's singing, but Benjamin was also a good student.

One day after *shalash sudis*, on Saturday Benjamin was back at Bekescsaba. They were singing at the table. After that came the Havdalah Service where you light the braided candle. Havdalah means separation because you say a prayer separating the holy day of Shabbat from the weekday. *Havdalah* is Hebrew for separation, separating the holiness from the secular. First comes the evening service, then the Havdalah. After the Havdalah, the students were given a test. The rabbi tested the students twice a week, once on the Talmud and a second time on Yoreh De'ah. The Yoreh De'ah test was given after the Havdalah. The rabbi asked the questions.

Benjamin said, "I don't know."

"What do you mean you don't know?"

Benjamin said, "I didn't study the Yoreh De'ah."

Benjamin made no excuse. He did not study it. Then the rabbi asked another question, and nobody knew the answer to it. Benjamin raised his hand. Benjamin gave him the correct answer.

The rabbi said, "How do you know this, you said you didn't study?"

Benjamin said, "I didn't study it, but I remember it from the lecture when you taught it."

So he said, "You know, you have a good brain without studying if you know this. How much better would you do if you really did study?"

He criticized Benjamin for not studying and at the same time complimented him for remembering his lectures.

Benjamin's younger brother was not ready to study at the yeshiva. Bekescsaba also had a Yeshiva, K'Tanah, a small yeshiva for younger boys. Benjamin had him accepted at the Yeshiva K'Tanah, where he did pretty well because he knew more than the other boys there. Chayim came from a house where they studied constantly. He tutored others, the weaker students, and sometimes the parents of the weaker students would pay him to tutor them, and so he had a little pocket money. Bekescsaba was a very good experience for Chayim, just like Sighet was for Benjamin when he was younger.

CHAPTER 17

While Benjamin was deep in his own thoughts, the jury was deep into their deliberations.

The concept of a jury trial is deeply ingrained in our American judicial system. The jury system can be traced back to June 15, 1215 in England, when King John signed the Magna Carta. The concept of "a jury of one's peers" comes from the Magna Carta. A jury trial consists of twelve strangers brought together to decide the fate of another stranger.

The Seventh Amendment to the United States Constitution states that: "In Suits at common law, where the value in controversy shall exceed twenty dollars, the right of trial by jury shall be preserved."

Article XV of the Massachusetts Constitution states that: "In all controversies concerning property, and in all suits between two or more persons, except in cases in which it has heretofore been otherways used and practiced, the parties have a right to a trial by jury; and this method of procedure shall be held sacred."

Benjamin's jury consisted of twelve strangers, seven women and five men. Not one person on that jury was one of Benjamin's peers. They all came with their own biases and prejudices. Would they cancel each other out and produce a fair result? Or would those biases affect the verdict and produce an unfair outcome?

A look at this jury reveals some interesting features. Frank Scott was thirty-three, a college graduate, who served in Iraq with the marines and the only African-American on the jury. He grew up in Selma, Alabama. As a child in Alabama, Frank suffered the indignities of being black. You never looked a white man in the eye. When they called you boy, you said, "yes sir." After high school he joined the Marines. When his tour of duty was over, he went to school at Northeastern University and graduated with a degree in Business Administration. Frank now works for a medium-sized high-tech company as their Business Manager. Frank would decide the case on the evidence.

Mary Donovan is a thirty-seven year old, secular Jew, married to John Donovan, an Irish Catholic, and the mother of three children. Mary was an only child and the daughter of deeply religious Jews. When Mary married out of the faith, it broke her father's heart. Within three years of her marriage to John, Mary's father died of a heart attack never living to see any of his grandchildren. Mary was a sure yes for Benjamin, but she was not about to tell anyone.

Catherine Malagucci was twenty-two years old, a Roman Catholic, and in her last year of college at Boston University. Although she had heard the story of the Jews being the Christ killers, she had friends who were Jewish. None were very religious. Catherine came from a small town in South Dakota and had no interaction with any Jews growing up. The few Jewish friends she had were ones she met in college. She would likely decide on the evidence, but she had a definite bias in favor of the Roman Catholic teacher. She had no knowledge of the Holocaust.

Barbara Rutten was twenty-six years old, a recent college graduate, and the mother of two children. She was Protestant but not very religious. Barbara graduated from Emerson College with a liberal arts degree. She was now a full-time mother and lived in a small cottage in Revere. Her two children were ages one and a half, a daughter, and three, a son. She was very upset that she was seated as a juror because of the cost of childcare. She was hoping for a short trial. She was angry and blamed Benjamin. She was definitely leaning against Benjamin.

Ralph Brunner was twenty-nine years old, a college graduate, and employed as a systems analyst at a local bank. He was not very religious. He was brought up in fairly religious home as a Roman Catholic, but unknown to his parents, he was abused by a priest when he was an altar boy. He was not too happy to be on the jury, but he would likely decide on the evidence.

Elizabeth Ocean was twenty-eight years old, a Southern Baptist, and the mother of one child. Elizabeth grew up in Knoxville, Tennessee. She moved to South Boston with her husband, who recently left her for another woman. She had no Jewish friends. She was very unhappy to be sitting on the jury. She had childcare for her six-year-old daughter because she worked fulltime, but she was concerned that her boss would hold it against her that she was not at work. She could not afford to lose her job. Elizabeth resented Benjamin. She reasoned that she was on the jury because of him. She was not about to find in Benjamin's favor unless the evidence was clear and convincing. That was not the burden of proof, but that did not make any difference to Elizabeth.

John Lynch was forty-seven, Irish Catholic, and currently unemployed. John lived in Charlestown with his wife and four children. He resented every minute on the jury. He wanted to be out looking for work instead of sitting in a courtroom because of some Jew. He was not likely to find in Benjamin's favor.

Sue Smith was forty-three years old, a Muslim, and the mother of six children. Sue Smith was not about to tell anyone she was a Muslim, nor was she ever going to find in Benjamin's favor.

Janet Wu was forty-eight years old and the mother of one child. Her parents came from a small village outside of Xian, China, but Janet was born in the United States. Her parents settled in Chinatown, but Janet moved to Roslindale when she got married. Her parents were Buddhists, but Janet did not follow any particular religion. Janet worked as a secretary for a small real estate company, and she did not mind serving on the jury. Her son was in his second year at M.I.T. Janet would base her decision on the evidence.

Tom Kham was fifty-three years old and a Buddhist. His family emigrated from Cambodia when Tom was three. He became an American citizen in his twenties. Tom worked as a taxicab driver and resented every minute of his jury service. Every hour in court was an hour less of income for his family. Tom would try to be fair, but he was not likely to find in Benjamin's favor. It was because of Benjamin that he was now in court wasting his time Tom thought.

Jose Hernandez was fifty-seven years old, Catholic, and a naturalized citizen from Mexico. Jose was living with his wife in Chelsea. His four children had moved out and were now on their own. Jose was a manager at a local Burger King. He was concerned that time out of work might affect his job. His assistant manager was American and only twenty-nine. Jose thought that he might be pushed out and replaced by his young assistant. Jose would likely decide the case on the merits, but he was clearly not happy to be on this jury.

Pat Stern was fifty-nine years and the oldest juror. She was unmarried. She was an agnostic but was brought up by Christian parents. She was a teacher in the Melrose school system. She taught English at the high school and was also the softball coach and the basketball coach for the girl's team. She played basketball and softball at Holy Cross College in Worcester. She was a lesbian, but this was known by only by her closest friends. She would decide the case based on the evidence.

Jurors, like everyone else, have their biases and prejudices. Discrimination cases are difficult to win. When it involves religious discrimination, it is even more difficult. And when the religion is Jewish, it is more difficult still. Most people blame the problems in the Middle East on the Jews.

CHAPTER 18

While the jurors were into their deliberations and deep into their thoughts, Benjamin was deep into his own thoughts. In the winter of 1944, Hungarian Jews managed to free a great Hasidic Rebbe from a Polish camp in Poland. He came from the town of Belz. The Belz rabbi was one of the giants. The Hungarian Jews paid a great ransom for him, and he came to Hungary. He later got a Visa to go to Switzerland and eventually ended up in Palestine.

Benjamin had to go to Hungary to see this rabbi. He took a night train and arrived safely in Budapest early Friday morning to see this great Rebbe, to shake hands with him, to be blessed by him. Budapest was packed with Jews from all over the country, even though these were really ugly times. The Jews sensed something evil was happening to their world. Some people knew what was going on in Poland, in Auschwitz. Benjamin did not. Benjamin would never forgive them for not telling him. Benjamin went to Budapest but could not get near the rabbi because it was too crowded. At about two or three a.m. Sunday morning, the Rebbe finished Shabbat service. He dragged out the Shabbat service to have more holy time. Benjamin did manage to see the Belz rabbi's brother, who was also a Rebbe. They were both going to Israel, Palestine in those days.

"Time for lunch," Sarah said to Benjamin, jolting Benjamin back to the present. "I can't believe the jury has been out for three days."

"What does this mean?" asked Benjamin. "Is this good or bad?"

"There's no way to tell," said Sarah.

"I don't understand. Why can't you tell me something?" Benjamin asked.

"There are so many reasons the jury could be taking this long. They may be deadlocked. They may be confused about the evidence. There is just no way to tell. All we can do is wait," Sarah explained.

"What is confusing? They fired me because I practice traditional Judaism. The school preferred a young attractive Catholic girl over an old Jew like me," Benjamin said.

"Try not to get discouraged. The case went in well, and hopefully, the jury will come back with a verdict for you," Sarah said. "Unless you want to come with me, I'll see you after lunch."

"No thanks. I'll stay here and eat my apple," Benjamin replied. Benjamin was afraid that there were no Jews on the jury and that the jury would find against him. The longer the jury took the more he was convinced that he would lose.

While Benjamin was eating his apple, the jurors were into their discussions and deliberations.

"I think he took advantage of the Jewish holidays," said Sue Smith. "He took off all those days. If I was running a school, I would rather have someone that took fewer days off."

"But if that was part of his religion, why should the school hold that against him?" said Frank Scott.

"The chairman of the school committee was Jewish. Why would he discriminate against another Jew?" said Catherine Malagucci. "Besides, what about the letter from the Anti-defamation League that found no religious discrimination."

"Are you saying that a Jew who marries a non-Jew is the same as an Orthodox Jew who marries a Jew?" said Mary Donovan. "Catholics and Protestants are always fighting, yet they're both Christians. What's the difference with that and Orthodox and Reformed Jews?" Mary was not about to reveal that she herself was Jewish.

"The school would have to pay more to keep Sharnofsky," said Barbara Rutten. "Why isn't that a good reason?"

"Sharnofsky was the better teacher," said Ralph Brunner. "If the school has to let a teacher go, shouldn't they keep the better teacher? I think they discriminated against him because he was an Orthodox Jew."

The jury did not know the horrors Benjamin faced in the concentration camps. The judge excluded all of Benjamin's history. "Too prejudicial and not relevant to the issues the jury has to decide," said the judge. "The only issue for them to decide was whether Mr. Sharnofsky was discriminated against because of his age and/or his religion. We do not want them to be swayed by bias, prejudice or sympathy."

While the jury was deliberating Benjamin's fate, Benjamin was deep in his own thoughts of a past so horrific that no one who did not live through it could even begin to understand.

PART TWO

"There may be times when we are powerless to prevent injustice, but there must never be a time when we fail to protest."

Eli Wiesel

CHAPTER 19

On March 17th, 1944, the Germans came in and occupied Hungary. Hungary was also an anti-Semitic state. It was a fascist state, but Benjamin did not know too much about politics until then.

Benjamin's whole world was shattered, not only his, but the whole Jewish community was shattered

Benjamin's older brother was in Szombathezy, which was very distant from where Benjamin was. He was in another yeshiva. He went to study with a rabbi with whom Benjamin's father studied when he was a yeshiva bocher.

March 17, 1944, was the day after Purim. Benjamin was living in Bekescsaba. The Germans marched in darkness. A terrible darkness fell upon all Hungarian Jews. The sun suddenly stopped shining for them. On March 17, 1944, overnight the Germans occupied Hungary. Hungary was an ally of Germany, so it was not occupied before. Benjamin heard that the Germans occupied Hungary because they were afraid as the Russians pushed westward that Hungary would not fight on their own soil. They would surrender. They had a good reason for thinking so because Hungary did have a communist regime at the end of the First World War for a short period. So not trusting completely his ally, Hitler occupied Hungary.

As soon as the news reached Benjamin, the Germans marched in. They were all scared to death. They knew that the Germans were imprisoning Jews. They had some notion that they were all in concentration camps. Killing, they did not dare think of. That they were imprisoned is what they assumed. They had this assumption from news that reached them.

The yeshiva dissolved immediately. Everybody went home. Benjamin got a cable to go home. Benjamin took the first train home with his younger brother. It was not a smart move because they were not too far from the Romanian border. Benjamin could have smuggled himself and brother into Romania where it was safe at that time, or they could have gone to Budapest where it was much easier to hide than in Benjamin's own hometown. In Budapest there was Wallenberg, the Swedish diplomat who saved thousands. In a large city you could get lost. If Benjamin had cut his ear locks and got a haircut like a gentile boy, he could have passed for a native. Benjamin spoke Hungarian almost like a native, and he could have gotten false identity papers, just like Benjamin's sister did.

Benjamin's sister Lea, who was twenty-two at the time, was in Budapest. She sent Benjamin the cable to go home. She sent Benjamin's brother in the other city a cable to go home, but she did not go home.

There was a terrible foreboding of horrors yet to come, a sense of fear that was palpable. Even though they did not know about Auschwitz, they knew about prison camps and forced labor. They should have known about Auschwitz too. The leadership knew. They did not tell them. Why were they not told? On an interview on Israeli television a couple of years ago they asked if he knew about Auschwitz, why didn't you tell everybody? He said it would have created chaos. Let there be chaos rather than to go to the slaughterhouse, thought Benjamin.

CHAPTER 20

Benjamin went home, and there was extreme poverty. The day after Passover, in 1944, Solotvyno became a ghetto. The entire town became a ghetto. They brought in all the Jews from the surrounding villages.

There was no way out and no place to go. Everybody had large families. Where do you put the people who are brought in? They were Jews in danger just like Benjamin's family. They were crowded into Benjamin's home and others in the town. They got their own ration. They came with whatever money they had. They left their town, and their first stop was at Solotvyno. They did not have to feed them, but they did give them a place to sleep and a place to cook. Some people slept outside. It was already spring.

They did nothing, absolutely nothing, every day, just being scared. There was no school. Since before Benjamin became a yeshiva boy, he did not play. The children might have played. Benjamin was not a child. Benjamin was almost sixteen. Benjamin was a young adult. Benjamin came from yeshiva. He studied Talmud. He studied serious stuff.

But he could not study because he was scared to death. What will happen, when will it happen, tomorrow, what will happen, what will happen? This went on for a few weeks, in the ghetto. During those times, they had to register and show citizenship. They kept them busy registering them. They had to wear the star of David. That did not bother them, wearing the star. So, they were identified as Jews. In Berlin, wearing a star bothered the German Jews. It meant people would stay away from them, or would spit on them, or persecute them with impunity.

Benjamin's family was not bothered that they wore a Jewish star because they were seen as Jews without the star. Their dress could not be mistaken for a non-Jew.

If they caught you not wearing the star, they had only one punishment. The Germans, as well as the Hungarian Fascists, they beat you up. That was the punishment. If they did not kill you, they beat you up. Now, during those few weeks in the ghetto -- all of Hungary already was "ghettoized." Eichmann was in charge of the logistics, arranging the transport of Jews to Auschwitz.

During those few weeks, there were all kinds of rumors. At one point there was a rumor that Canada would take the Jews in. The Germans wanted to get rid of the Jews. They just wanted the Jews to relax so they would follow the orders and be taken to Auschwitz. They did not want any trouble. They did not want any chaos. They did not want any resistance, because the Jews could have resisted them. There were not that many armed men. Had they known where they were going, they could have resisted. There may have been a blood bath, but most would have survived. Not only would they have resisted, every town would have. All Hungarian Jews would have resisted if the leadership had told them.

In Benjamin's town there were two transports to leave the ghetto. They evacuated the ghetto. Half of the ghetto went on the first transport and the other half went on the second transport. The first transport went on a Friday. They met in a field to be counted and lined up, in a field that holds perhaps a thousand people, an open field in the village. You did not have to go very far to find the open field. From there people left their homes and took whatever they could, their money, their jewelry. Some buried their jewelry thinking they would one day return. They were told nothing, except that they were being resettled.

They were put in the ghetto for about six weeks. Then the transports came. The first transport passed by Benjamin's house on the main street. They brought them from the field, and they brought them past Benjamin's house up a hill towards the train, and Benjamin watched. Benjamin did not see them get on the train. Benjamin saw them marching with the bundles, with the kids. Benjamin saw the rabbi. He had his beard cut very short. He used to have a full beard. All his life he never cut his beard. He came from a Polish rabbinical family. He had his beard cut. Benjamin saw him, his wife, and his children. It was a very sad scene, and there was crying and wailing. It was a preview for Benjamin because Benjamin knew the next transport he would be in the same spot going up, marching up to the train.

The first transport left on Friday, and Benjamin and his family left the following Tuesday. Tuesday morning they reported to that open field area. Some Hungarian police beat up two boys from a family, for no reason at all. They beat them up, bloodied them, and you could not do anything. Who could do anything but watch in horror? At the time when you are already imprisoned by the guards you have no rights any more, and these two policemen, they were called border police. They beat up these two guys. They were teenage brothers. Benjamin knew the boys. One was about eighteen and the other was sixteen. Benjamin knew them well. Benjamin knew the house where they lived.

When they marched Benjamin to the transport, he thought, *I'm never going to come back here again!*

They marched up the hill to the train, Benjamin's parents and six siblings. Benjamin's oldest sister stayed in Budapest, the one that sent them the cable.

Benjamin's older brother was already in a concentration camp. He got the same cable that Benjamin got to go home, so he took a train home, the next day after the Germans marched in, but he had to change trains in Budapest. The Hungarian Nazis, including German soldiers, raided the railway station. Benjamin's brother was to change trains. He came from Upper Hungary. In order to go home, he had to change trains in Budapest. He was caught and arrested on the platform in the main Budapest railway station. No one knew what happened to him until later.

They spent the Passover, all these weeks without knowing where Benjamin's brother was. He just disappeared. They found out a few weeks later. At one point they released the boys under twelve. So Benjamin's brother asked one of those boys to tell Benjamin's family that he was alive, but not for long. The brother went to Auschwitz from there. He probably went with the very first transport from Hungary to Auschwitz.

The transport had 60 to 70 boxcars, not passenger cars. There were about 3500 people loaded on the train. The train was used for cattle, but now they were using it for the Jews. There were two little windows on each side of each car, about 12-14 inches wide, to let air in for the cattle. Those were little windows closed with barbed wire.

It was about May 20, 1944. It was already warm. They took a whole community, old, young, rabbis, doctors, lawyers, teachers, infants, the sick. They took out the sick from the hospital and brought them to the train. Those in the hospital were not allowed to remain free. Every Jew was taken. From the hospitals they brought them to the train. If they could not walk, they were carried.

This act, this experience of taking an entire community, on a train is unimaginable. Everybody from a day old child to a 90 year old, everybody, all professions, young, rich and old, and they put 70 or 80 of them in a boxcar, where you did not have enough air to breath or room to sit down.

Each boxcar had two buckets. One was to serve as a bathroom. It was curtained off with a blanket, in a corner. Somebody curtained it off. The train made many stops. At each of the stops somebody would empty the bucket. The other bucket was for drinking water. One bucket of water for 70 people. You could not drink to satisfaction. There were only a few gallons of water for everyone so the water was rationed.

The train stopped because military trains had priority, and they had to wait for the line to clear. So they would go for two hours and stop for four, five or six hours sometimes.

They did not have much food before they got on the train. There was a famine in Hungary, in Benjamin's part of Hungary, very little food, but each person was given a small amount of food. You were given a certain amount of flour before you got on the train. They were given nothing to eat on the train.

They were on this train for three days and three nights. At the time, to add to their terror, no one knew how long they would be on this train or where they were going. They never got off the train during those three days. They slept sitting down. They took turns because they could not all sit down at the same time. There was not enough room.

Although they were on the train for three days and three nights, Benjamin does not remember a word that was spoken. What do people talk about in such a situation? They had to talk. They were talking, but Benjamin did not retain a word about what they talked about.

Benjamin remembers his father wrapped in his prayer shawl and praying and praying and praying like there was no tomorrow, and for him there was no tomorrow. The train finally stopped. Benjamin did not remember seeing his mother get off the train, although they were on the same train. When the train stopped, Benjamin knew they had arrived. For most of the passengers it was their final destination.   Benjamin could see the camp, Auschwitz, or what was called Birkenau, Auschwitz. He saw the barracks. There was a big sign at the gate that read "Arbeit Macht Frei." "Work makes you free."   The sign should have read, "Lasciate ogne speranza, voi ch'intrate."   "Abandon all hope, ye who enter here."

CHAPTER 21

The doors opened, and a number of prisoners came toward the train. These prisoners were called kapos, an Italian word meaning head. They were there to maintain order. There were some Jewish kapos, some German kapos. There were many German prisoners also in the camps. Communists were in the camps, homosexuals, and anyone the Germans considered undesirable. These kapos in stripped clothing came toward the train. There were fifty or sixty of them lined up. There were German soldiers with guns and dogs, surrounding the train. The doors were opened, and the German soldiers were screaming out orders, in five or six different languages.

They screamed out the same orders, "Get off the train, fast, fast, fast." This was always repeated three times. "Get off the train, fast, fast, fast, and leave everything behind you, take nothing with you." So whatever belongings they took and thought they were going to have wherever and when they were going to be resettled was left on the train. They got off the train with only the clothes they had on their backs.

They were already beating people as soon as they opened the doors. The kapos and the Germans beat people who maybe did not step the right way or asked them a question or something. They beat people in order to terrorize them, and they gave the orders, leave everything behind you. After the prisoners got off the train, the German soldiers ordered the women and children to form a line or a column alongside the train. There was chaos. Some people were too old to get off. The sick people were taken on stretchers behind the train and taken to the gas chambers.

Benjamin was in a state of mind that was indescribable. There were a lot of people looking for family members. Mothers looking for their children. Children looking for their mothers. Everyone was told to be quiet and move forward to the end of the train.

Then Benjamin could see something happening in front of him but did not know what because it was so far he could not see.

As he got closer, he saw German soldiers or officers in front like a welcoming committee. They were very polite. They did not want any trouble on that platform. The so-called "welcoming committee" consisted of German soldiers and one special officer whose name Benjamin did not know until the next day. His name was Doctor Josef Mengele. Benjamin could see that Dr. Mengele was separating the people. He was showing with his finger to go to the left or to the right. He sent most of the people to the left. He sent only a handful of young men and young women to the right. Benjamin was trying to figure out what he was doing. How did he decide where to send the people?

Although Benjamin had not eaten much in several days and was stuffed in a boxcar and was in a weakened condition, his mind was working very fast because he was in danger. It soon became apparent to Benjamin that Dr. Mengele was sending to his right where the camp was, only young men and young women, and not all young men and young women. The rest, about 85%, were being sent to his left, to the other side of the tracks away from the camp.

There was so much chaos that Benjamin never saw his mother or little sisters get off the train. Benjamin's father and his younger brother, the one that was with him in the yeshiva, were right behind Benjamin in an enormous line of people.

As Benjamin came closer, he saw a Hungarian woman, a young mother in her early 20's with an infant in her arms. The soldiers took away the infant and handed the infant to somebody assigned to go to the right of Dr. Mengele to the camp. The mother started screaming in Hungarian, "I want to go with my baby." The soldiers looked at Dr. Mengele, and he nodded yes. So she went with her baby to the left. That was just before Benjamin's turn came.

A few seconds later Benjamin was standing in front of Dr. Mengele, and he stopped Benjamin and asked in German, "Wie alt sind sie?" Benjamin did not know German, but he knew Yiddish. Yiddish is half German, so Benjamin understood. "Wie alt sind sie?" "How old are you?" Benjamin said 18, and Benjamin was sent to the side he wanted to go, the right. He did not want to go to the other side. The people that went to the other side were older women, children, the elderly, and the sick.

Benjamin was not even 16, but he said he was 18. He had not prepared his answer. It was as if an angel had whispered in Benjamin's ear, "Say 18." Benjamin had never lied about his age. Benjamin was ordered to run behind the others and ordered not to look back. He never saw his father or brother who was behind him. Had Benjamin said he was 15 or 16, he might not have been sent to the right, and Benjamin's story would never have been told.

CHAPTER 22

Just as Sarah came back from lunch, the courtroom clerk called out in the hallway, "The Jury has a question. Please return to the courtroom."

Benjamin, Sarah, and the others went back into the courtroom.

"All rise, the court is now in session," the court officer stated as the judge came into the courtroom. After the judge took his seat, the court officer then said, "You may now be seated."

"The jury has another question," said the judge. "The question is, 'Is it discrimination if the school committee let Benjamin go to save money, since the younger teacher who was retained cost less money?' How do you want me to answer that question? Let me ask plaintiff's counsel first. What do you say?"

"Yes it is," said Sarah. "Teachers who have taught longer will generally be older and will be paid more. So there will be an impact on age discrimination."

"But there would be no impact on religious discrimination, right?" the judge stated.

"This is not about saving money. This is about picking a younger, Catholic less-qualified teacher over a better qualified, older teacher, who practiced traditional Judaism," asserted Sarah.

"What do you say?" asked the judge looking in the direction of defense counsel.

"School committees should be able to save money and that should not be considered age or religious discrimination," said Ralph Simon.

"I agree with that," said the judge. "As long as they picked the younger teacher to save money and not to discriminate against the plaintiff because of his age or religion, that is a lawful, non-discriminatory reason."

"I object!" Sarah stated.

"Objection noted," said the Judge.

Sarah took Benjamin aside outside the courtroom.

"What does this mean?" Benjamin asked.

"I think this judge is screwing you," she said. "The judge is handing the case to the school committee."

"What can we do?" asked Benjamin.

"We can appeal. The judge has made a number of legal errors," Sarah said.

"Do we have any chance? I can't believe this! I survived the Nazis only to lose to an American jury! How can this be!?" Benjamin implored.

"There's always a chance, but it doesn't look good," Sarah replied. All we can do is sit and wait."

Benjamin alone with his thoughts drifted back in time.

The afternoon after they arrived they showered. Three days later Benjamin found out what happened to most of the people on the train. Benjamin's mother was sent to the other side. He never saw his mother again. Benjamin's three little sisters went to the other side. He never saw his sisters again. Benjamin's father and younger brother were sent to the other side. He never saw them again.

In Auschwitz, the first thing they did was remove all your hair. They used clippers to cut all hair. The blades were dull, and it was very painful. The few young women sent to the right were separated and sent somewhere else, leaving only the men. Benjamin never saw those women again.

The men were sent into a huge room to undress for a shower. There were hooks with numbers over them. They told the men to make sure they remembered where they left their clothing, and then they were sent into the showers. They were all showering at the same time for a minute or two. They were given a piece of soap, but no towel. When they finished showering, instead of going back through the door where they left their clothing, they were sent out another door. Their clothing they never saw again.

Benjamin was given his new wardrobe fit for a prisoner in a concentration camp - a striped jacket and striped pants. There was also a striped shirt of a little thinner material and a cap of the same material. Benjamin was also given wooden clogs. That is what they gave him. No socks, no underwear, no toothbrush. He did not have to brush his teeth. He was subhuman.

Benjamin was placed in a single building with 500 other inmates. In the First World War the building was a stable for horses. Now, it was a barracks for 500 men. The barracks were long and narrow.

They were given nothing to eat or drink. The Germans, the kapos, those who gave orders advised them not to drink the water. There was typhoid. There was cholera. There were all kinds of diseases in the water. All of Benjamin's family that came with him on the transport were murdered the first day, except for one first cousin. His name was Simcha. He was about a year older than Benjamin. They slept in bunks with bare boards. There was no pillow and no straw on the bare boards. The whole barracks was filled with bunks. There was a narrow corridor in the middle from one end of the barracks to the other. There were bunks on each side. They put six people on a bunk, eighteen in a three-tier bunk for a total of about five hundred men. Benjamin slept next to his cousin Simcha and talked half the night about where they were. The next day they took Benjamin out and put him into a youth barrack. He never saw his cousin again. The cousin did not survive. He perished in the camps.

They asked all those who were under 18. Benjamin raised his hand thinking that he might be taken to a better camp if he was under 18.

Auschwitz was divided into different camps, subdivided with wires. You could not move from one camp to another or from one subdivision to another. If you were in one camp, that is where you were. Benjamin thought that there were 10 or 20 subdivisions, maybe more, but he was not sure because he never saw the whole camp.

A typical day while Benjamin was at Auschwitz was he did nothing. He was not put to work. He was not locked up. He could go outside the barracks. He could walk. He had to be there for the *appels*[15], and he had to be there to sleep.

Benjamin was put in the *jugendliche*[16] block. A barracks was called a block. There were about 1200 kids in two blocks, 600 in each bock. Most of them were from Hungary, from recent transports, and from Benjamin's transport. There were two kids Benjamin knew. One was the brother of Benjamin's best friend, who was just thirteen. This younger brother was so lost. It was

---

[15] Roll-call

[16] Youth or teenager.

the first time he had been away from his mother, his parents. Benjamin had already been away from his parents for three years, so he was more mature. Benjamin's best friend did not make it. His whole family perished.

CHAPTER 23

Benjamin also knew one boy he had befriended in the Solotvyno ghetto and who had lived in Benjamin's house during the ghetto weeks. His name was Isaac. So they stayed together that first night, nothing to eat and nothing to drink.

They woke them up at four o'clock in the morning to stand for *appel*. They were lined up in rows of five, one behind the other and counted. You could be standing for an hour or longer in the cold, early in the morning with little clothing. After a couple of hours of standing in the *appel*, they were given breakfast.

The breakfast consisted of a little coffee, not real coffee, more like black water. The coffee was in a large bowl. The first one in line drank a few sips, and then it was handed to the next one behind him, then to the next, and the next. Benjamin was usually in the back of the line, so he had very little to drink. That was his breakfast.

For lunch hour he was given some kind of soup. It appeared to contain some kinds of root vegetables, like parsnips and maybe a few carrots, made into a soup. It was not edible. It had a stench. You had to hold your nose to get a few spoons down your throat. You had to put something in your stomach. You could not finish it, no matter how hungry you were. It was that bad.

In the evening after the *appel*, Benjamin was given some more of that "coffee" and a piece of bread for his dinner. On Sundays, in addition to the coffee and the bread, they were given a tiny piece of margarine and a thin slice of salami, very, very thin, maybe half an inch. That is how Benjamin lived for three weeks.

Benjamin and his friend Isaac always stayed together. Those first three weeks they were in the Zigeuner lager.[17] One section was for the gypsies. Hitler killed many German gypsies. There were a barracks on each side and a street in the middle. There was a street where they could come with trucks and take you away.

---

[17] The Gypsy camp.

On each side there were barracks lined up. There were certain times you could walk. There were not too many regular prisoners there. There were mostly gypsies and kids.

In front of the camp there was a barracks with people who unloaded the trains when the prisoners got off. They were called the Canada group. While unloading the train, they would find some food, some cookies, and marmalade, little jars. They snuck it into the camp in their pockets. The Germans probably did not care. If they cared, the Germans would have stopped it. The Canada group would give the kids some of the stuff that they snuck in, so that augmented their intake of food. They would give them a couple of cookies or a little marmalade. This was more valuable than gold.

One day while Benjamin and his friend were walking toward the Canada group for some food, a prisoner on the left side of the street called Benjamin over to him in Yiddish.

"When did you arrive?"

Benjamin said "Three days ago."

He said, "Yes, I can see that you are newcomers because you still have some color in your cheeks. Where are you coming from, Hungary?"

"Yes," Benjamin replied.

The prisoner knew of the Hungarian transports. All the transports that were coming during those weeks were from Hungary. One reason the Germans occupied Hungary was they were afraid that Hungary would surrender to the Russians. Another reason was that here were close to a million Jews still free in Hungary. The war was being lost. Hitler could not stand letting a million Jews survive. He came in for the Jews. The troops marched in without firing a shot. Hungary did not resist. Adolf Eichmann came behind the troops in one of the limousines, and he set up shop in Budapest to annihilate all the Hungarian Jews.

The man Benjamin spoke to was a Polish Jew. Although he spoke in Yiddish, it was Polish Yiddish. Hungarian Yiddish and Polish Yiddish are slightly different. He called Benjamin and his friend into his office. He had a little office in the barracks. He was in charge of that barracks, and the one who distributed the food there. He brought them into his office and sat them down in chairs. It would be more than a year before Benjamin would again sit on a chair.

He then asked, "Where are your parents?"

Benjamin said, "Our parents were sent to the other camp."

The man sat quietly for a while. He could not look them in the eyes.

Then he started shaking his head and he said, "No, no, no, there is no other camp over there. Better learn it fast. This is Auschwitz. This is a camp where people are brought for extermination. I won't survive. Nobody in Auschwitz will survive. All those who went to the other side were killed within two hours. They are already in ashes. You have no more parents. Forget about your parents. Concentrate on one thing, on survival. The first thing you have to do to survive is to get out of the children's block."

Benjamin's blood ran cold.

He said, "Auschwitz is the worst place on this planet, and the *kinder blocken*[18] where you are is the worst place in Auschwitz because you are there only for a temporary stay. They keep the kids there for show, for the record, to show some journalist that they have children here. They want the world to think they are not killing children."

Benjamin asked, "What are you saying that they are killing everybody here?"

"Yes. Every few weeks they take these kids, they bring trucks and take them to the gas chambers and re-fill the barracks with new youngsters from the new arrivals, with still some color in their cheeks."

When he learned that his whole family had been wiped out, Benjamin was in shock. He did not feel anything. He did not cry. He did not say a word. Neither did Benjamin's friend. Suddenly, they were not humans any more. Suddenly, they were much worse off than they could ever imagine. They were already so traumatized that this news about the killing that went on just added to their trauma. They were in shock. They did not react at all.

He said, "The only way to survive is to escape, but from Auschwitz nobody escapes."

---

[18] The Children's block.

He was wrong about that.   Two young Jewish boys from Slovakia did escape about a year before, but he did not know that.

He said, "First you have to get out of the children's barracks. Then when you are in a barracks with adults, you might be shipped out to some other camp, maybe you will work in the fields." Jews were not put to work in the fields.   Some Gentiles were. But he did not know that.

Benjamin and his friend spent three weeks in the *kinder blocken*. Finally, the chance came for some of them to get out.

CHAPTER 24

One afternoon during *appel* the guards screamed out a notice. They always yelled or screamed. They never spoke. They screamed out a notice, "All those over eighteen should raise their hand, all those over eighteen." The children all raised their hands, thirteen year olds, fourteen year olds. By that time, three weeks in the camp, they all knew what was awaiting them.

The next day they brought about a half dozen doctors, prison doctors. They were Polish Jews who also could spoke perfect German. They were prisoner doctors. They had some white coat to identify them as medical men, and they set up little tables, like card tables and a couple of chairs. The children were lined up just like a regular *appel*. The doctors were seated. They had no instruments. They just had pencils and papers, and some of the children were called out individually to come before the doctor, and the doctor was to decide whether the child was strong enough to go to work. They needed fifty-three people to complete a transport out, so they came to the children's barracks to pick out the fifty-three oldest and strongest. Benjamin was a short sixteen year old, but he stood on a rock to make himself look taller. He was called out, and the doctor looked at Benjamin and Benjamin's hands.

"Have you worked before?" he asked.

Benjamin said, "Yes."

"What kind of work?" he asked

Benjamin said, "Farm work. My grandfather had a farm, and I worked on his farm."

He looked at Benjamin's hands. Those hands never worked. Those hands had only touched the pages of the Talmud. But, Benjamin was selected as one of the fifty-three, as was Benjamin's friend Isaac. So again they were together. They were immediately taken to another barracks for that night, and in the morning they were shipped out. They took them to a train with boxcars. This time there were only about thirty people in the boxcar. They were comfortable in the boxcars, not like before.

Benjamin was being transported with mostly adults in their twenties and in their thirties. They could sit down in the train, quite comfortably, and it was not a long ride, about one night and one day. They never told them where they were going. They had no food to eat. They had no water to drink. They only had one bucket for waste.

They arrived in a small market town in Austria called Mauthausen. Outside of the town there was a camp on a hill. They were marched through the town where there were houses. Outside the town there was a big mountain and a quarry where the prisoners worked. They marched up on the left side of the quarry. It was quite steep, and at the top was a huge camp. Mauthausen was the central camp in Austria. From Mauthausen you would be assigned to one of the other sub camps in Austria.

When Benjamin arrived at Mauthausen, he was given a shower. It was only his second shower since he had left his home almost a month ago. The first shower was in Auschwitz. In Mauthausen Benjamin was given a shower and a clean uniform. He went into an office and, standing in a line, he was registered. They asked for your name, hometown, your birthday, and you were given a number. After you were registered you were not called by your name, but by your number. Benjamin's number was 74898. The number was not stamped on Benjamin's arm as they did in Auschwitz. They gave him a bracelet, and the number was stamped on the bracelet tied to his wrist with a wire. Benjamin was not given a tattoo number in Auschwitz because he was supposed to be killed later on. You were tattooed when they designated you to go to work. That is why Benjamin did not get tattooed in Auschwitz, but he did get a number at Mauthausen.

At Mauthausen the food was the same as in Auschwitz, the same terrible stinking soup. Isaac was with Benjamin at Mauthausen. They got out together. He was one of the fifty-three boys, and they were together in the same car. They kept together. When they took a shower, they were next to each other. They were at Mauthausen one night. The next day they were shipped off to Melk. Melk was one of the satellite camps. Benjamin went with Isaac to Melk. Melk was a couple of hours more or less by train from Mauthausen.

Melk is a small beautiful town on the Danube River. It is famous for the Melk Abbey built between 1702 and 1736.

Benjamin was able to see this abbey as he passed through the town. The Melk camp was outside the town on top of a hill.

There were roughly ten thousand people at this camp. The camp was a military training camp that was turned into a concentration camp. Some of the buildings were made of bricks, but in order to accommodate the ten thousand people, wooden barracks were added.

One of the barracks was called the revier.[19] No medicine was practiced there. They had no medications. While there were doctors there, the only supplies were bandages. If you were hurt, they could bandage you up, but nothing else. If you were too sick to work, you would be put in the revier to die. If you had a high enough fever, you would be put in the revier and put on a narrow cot with two or three others. If your temperature went down, you were released. Very few people ever came out alive. Most of them caught other illnesses from the others in the revier who were dying from typhus or other diseases. There was a lot of typhus in the camp because there were a lot of flies.

---

[19] A *revier* (abbreviated from German *Krankenrevier*, or "sick bay") in the language of Nazi camps was a barrack for sick concentration camp inmates. Most of the medical personnel were inmates themselves.

CHAPTER 25

When Benjamin arrived in Melk, he stood up for the *appel* in the yard of the camp. The camp had a big yard. From that yard Benjamin and his friend Isaac were assigned to Barrack Five. The barracks was a brick building built for soldiers and not for prisoners, so it had rooms, but not large rooms, rooms. Each room had thirty to forty people sleeping in three tier bunks. There were some straw mats, and each prisoner was each given a thin blanket.

There was one entrance gate to the Melk camp with electrified fences all around the camp. Benjamin did not go to work the first couple of days. He hid under his bunk. Isaac went to work. Isaac did not know that Benjamin was hiding. Benjamin did not know why he was not missed at work. Benjamin decided he better go to work. He was afraid that if he was caught that they would beat him to death.

The first day Benjamin lined up for work he was hit from behind with a rubber stick right in the middle of his head. Benjamin thought his head was split into two halves, like two halves of a walnut. It was terribly painful. Benjamin found out a couple of days later that he was hit by a French kapo.

The French kapo asked, "Did it hurt you?"

Benjamin said, "Of course."

"I had to hit you. They were watching me," he said.

He had come to apologize. He did not mean to hit Benjamin so hard, but that was part of his job, to beat the prisoners, to keep people in line.

Benjamin's first assignment was road construction. He was taken on a truck with ten or fifteen other workers. It was an open truck that was run on coal. Benjamin was forced to sit on the back of the truck, and he could not tolerate the fumes. He was sick for days and almost died. Fortunately, he only went twice. Then he was assigned to one of the main work shifts.

Most of the people in the Melk camp, about seventy-five hundred, worked in Schachtbau. There were three shifts for the

Schachtbau project, roughly twenty-five hundred for each shift, working around the clock.

The prisoners were marched down to the train out of the Melk camp through the front gate and in lines of five with soldiers on each side with a weapon at the ready. The soldiers were not more than two or three feet away from each other ready to shoot. On the left side of the hill there was this beautiful countryside. The prisoners were not taken to the main train station. They were taken to a ramp away from the main station and would wait on the ramp for a train to take them to the work site. Although they were placed in boxcars, they were not crowded. The train took about eight or ten minutes to get to the Schachtbau construction site.

During that short train ride, they went through a tunnel for about a minute or so. The doors were open on both sides of the boxcar with a guard on each door. When they came out of the tunnel, there was this huge construction site.

They were digging tunnels, not for transportation, not for roads, not for trains. They were digging tunnels for bunkers, for protection. They dug in this large, stone, mountain with those little electric jackhammers that construction people use for building roads.

After that assignment, Benjamin was then assigned to do shoveling. This consisted of shoveling sand and stone onto a conveyor belt that would carry it out. The shovels were large; the size of snow shovels and very heavy. You had to fill the shovel and work quickly. If you did not fill the shovel or work fast enough, the kapos would hit you. That was their job.

German soldiers were also around. They were moving around, constantly moving, overseeing, to make sure the kapos did their jobs. The kapos' job was to beat the workers when they were not working or when they were not working fast enough. There were three shifts, 7 a.m. to 3 p.m., 3 p.m. to 11 p.m., and 11 p.m. to 7 a.m. Benjamin worked an eight-hour shift thirteen days in a row. They were off every second Sunday, but that second Sunday was no big deal either because they would make them do all kinds of other things in the camp. The Germans did not let the prisoners rest.

Chapter 26

In order to be at the 7 a.m. shift, they would wake you at 4:30 a.m. They would feed you breakfast. Breakfast would consist of what they called coffee and a wedge of bread. It was a round piece of bread cut into eight slices, and you would get one piece. They would also do an *appel* when you left and an *appel* when you returned. You also had to wait for the train to take you to the construction site.

They were building tunnels so that the Germans could manufacture arms underground. When they finished digging one tunnel, they started a second tunnel, and a third tunnel. Then they dug tunnels interconnecting the tunnels creating a whole complex underground. When the complex was finished, the Germans brought in machinery to manufacture arms. The prisoners were helping the war effort. The tunnels were built to protect the German's manufacture of arms. There were German civilians and engineers in the complex. Although the Germans were not supposed to talk to the prisoners, some of them did. The soldiers could not watch every square inch. The German civilians would talk to some of the prisoners and give them some news, but they never talked about what was happening with the war.

Benjamin saw the Germans bringing in the machines but never saw them working on the machines. Once the tunnel began manufacturing arms the prisoners were not allowed inside.

Benjamin soon found out that about fifteen or twenty youngsters were doing an easier job called *spitzen traeger*. A *spitz* in German is a point. *Traeger* means carriers of these points. These were the long, steel bits used in the jackhammer. They were about twelve inches long. There is a bit put in and tightened, and you need to sharpen it in order to dig. If you dig for a while, it becomes dull. The job of the *spitzen traeger* was to collect the dull bits and take them outside the tunnels to the person outside who was making them sharp. That was Benjamin's new job. He would carry about ten or twelve *spitzen* in a little wire carrying case outside to have them sharpened. After they were sharpened, he would bring them back to put on the jackhammers.

The chief kapo on one of the shifts was a German gypsy. He would line up the twenty-five hundred people on the shift and give the men instructions and divide them into different work groups. When he called out the *spitzen traeger* group, Benjamin lined up with that group. Nobody assigned him to that group. Benjamin thought it looked like an easy job, so he just lined up with the group. No one said a word. So just like that Benjamin became a *spitzen traeger*. As a *spitzen traeger*, Benjamin had a relatively easy job. The Germans and the kapos that were on the work site treated the *spitzen traeger* very lightly. They did not bother them. They could sit down and rest or sit down and talk. They were privileged because they were youngsters. It was known that this gypsy *kapo* liked youngsters.

Once you became a *spitzen traeger* you had these privileges. At night sometimes you would make a little fire outside, and the Germans would go by, the soldiers and kapos, and they would not bother the *spitzen traegers*. An adult could not do this.

The food was better in Melk. Benjamin was given coffee and bread in the morning, and an eighth wedge of bread and coffee in the evening after work. Benjamin was usually given something to go with the bread, often a little cottage cheese and sometimes marmalade. Twice a week he would be given some margarine and a piece of salami. There was also soup, but it was awful, similar to the soup in Auschwitz. In the winter of 1944 Benjamin was told that food was going to improve, that they were going to get the same food as the soldiers. Although Benjamin did not believe this, the food did improve. Benjamin did not know if it was the same level of the soldiers, but the soup improved. They gave them three or four boiled potatoes. They gave them macaroni soup on some Sundays. They did not get the kind of meat that the soldiers received, but the food improved enough that you would not die from starvation in Melk. The food was good by concentration camp standards. Sometimes they would be given a double ration of bread. Instead of an eighth of bread, some days they were given a quarter of bread in the morning and a quarter of bread in the evening.

Benjamin was in block number five with Isaac. Each bunk had three tiers. Benjamin was on the top. The youngsters always were on top because it was easier for them to climb up than it was for the older people. Under Benjamin, in the middle tier, was a Doctor Adler, a Romanian Jew. He did not practice medicine in the camp. He was a laborer. There were lawyers, doctors, and engineers. It did not matter. Everybody was a laborer.

One day during the first few weeks in the camp, Dr. Adler sat down with Benjamin and Isaac, and said, "I know what they are doing here. They are slowly killing us. They are making us work very hard. They give us less calories than you expend, and we are in deficit, every day we are in deficit. That's how we are all going to die, slowly. They are killing us off. So I advise you to conserve energy. Conserve every drop of energy that you can conserve. When you come back to the camp from work, don't walk around, because you are wasting energy. In fact, you shouldn't walk when you can sit. You shouldn't sit when you can lie down. This way the accumulation of energy, calories that you are saving may make a big difference in the end, because most of us are going to die here. In order to stretch out the time so you are not one of those who dies four weeks before liberation, you should take measures to conserve your energy."

They never gave the prisoners enough time to sleep. As a *spitzen traeger*, Benjamin could walk off from work and find a place to sleep in the tunnels, under machinery. So to conserve energy, Benjamin would sleep a couple of hours each day. He would go to sleep at two in the morning and come back at four and nobody missed him. Benjamin would give the workers extra sharp bits so that their work would not be affected if he was gone for two hours.

This went on for five nights. Then one morning, Benjamin overslept. He did not have a watch. Nobody did. Benjamin did not have the sense to tell a friend to wake him up. So he overslept. When they blew the whistle at 7:00 a.m. for everybody to get out of the tunnels, Benjamin did not hear the whistle. He was about two or three feet under a water pump. He could not be seen nor could he hear the whistle sound. They counted the shift. When they counted the night shift, Benjamin was missing. They counted and recounted. They beat the people trying to get someone to tell them about the missing person. They thought it was an escape attempt.

CHAPTER 27

They searched the tunnels but could not find Benjamin. At 9:30 a.m. Benjamin finally woke up. He did not know it was 9:30 a.m., but he woke up and looked outside the tunnel. He saw the sun and knew he was in trouble. When Benjamin walked out of the tunnel, a kapo grabbed him and blew the whistle as a sign that the missing person was found. The kapo started beating Benjamin. Then the kapo handed Benjamin over to the chief kapo who started beating Benjamin. Then the soldiers beat him with shovels and fists. Benjamin passed out. They put Benjamin on a stretcher and took him back to camp. The entire two shifts were held up until they found Benjamin.

The *lagerfuhrer* was in charge of the camp. He was an SS officer and did not live at the camp, but he came for the six o'clock evening *appel*. This is the most important *appel*. All the prisoners would line up and wait for the *lagerfuhrer* to arrive. The prisoners could stand for hours until he arrived. They could see him come by car and stop at the entrance of the gate. When the *lagerfuhrer* came into the camp he would go directly to the camp secretary. The camp secretary would shout out an oral report so everyone could hear. The camp secretary would tell the *lagerfuhrer* how many prisoners were in line, how many were at work, how many were in the reviere, and how many had died since yesterday. The prisoners knew how many had died each day. Sixty or seventy people died on any particular day. In the colder winter months it would be in the nineties. Ninety-eight people were the most people Benjamin remembers dying on any particular day.

They did not die from starvation. They died from diseases, but also from not wanting to live that miserable existence any longer. There was no medical care. If you got an infection that could have been cured, you would die from that. The prisoners' bodies and clothing were full of lice. The lice would give the prisoners typhus. The lice would go right under the first level of skin and stay there. Benjamin had no more than six showers in Melk. They would disinfect the clothing while they were taking their shower. Every item of clothing had the prisoner's number on it, so when they finished their showers, their clothes would be returned. This was supposed to kill the lice, but it did not. A couple of days later the lice would return. Lice were a big problem. People died and the living envied the dead. Their suffering was over.

Benjamin was taken back to the camp on a stretcher. The French kapo who had earlier hit Benjamin in the head woke Benjamin up while Benjamin was lying on the stretcher just as they arrived in camp.

He said to Benjamin, "Listen we are going to arrive soon in the camp. You tell them the truth."

The *lagerfuhrer* had the rank of Obersturmfuhrer. He only arrived at camp at six o'clock in the evening, but as soon as they could not find Benjamin, they called the *lagerfuhrer*. He did not come to the camp. It was all done by phone.

The French kapo told Benjamin, "If you lie to them, you will be in big time trouble. Tell them the truth that you fell asleep."

Once they arrived back at the camp the rest of the shift of the twenty-five hundred people had their breakfast and went to their bunks. Benjamin was taken off the stretcher and put next to the electrified wire. He was forced to stand there. They did not tell him how long he had to stand there. He was about a foot away from the electrified wire and a couple of feet from the guardhouse. The guard watched Benjamin, and Benjamin watched the guard. It was late August and was very hot. Benjamin was dirty and bloody from the beatings.

CHAPTER 28

Benjamin was bloodied and wanted very badly to go to the washroom to wash up a little, to get rid of the blood and freshen up a little bit, so he raised his hand. The guard was about eight feet away from Benjamin at his little post at the gate.

He asked, "What do you want?"

Benjamin said, "I need to go to the bathroom." He did not have to go to the bathroom. Benjamin's stomach was empty, but he wanted to wash up, so he used that as an excuse.

"I need to go, you can't let me stand here," Benjamin said.

"Scheys en dein hosen," he said "Shit it in your pants."

Benjamin could do nothing. This was about eleven o'clock in the morning. At twelve the guard had some little sandwiches for lunch.

He stretched out his hand to Benjamin with a sandwich and asked, "Are you hungry?"

Benjamin who was starving said, "Yes."

"Do you want some?" he asked.

Benjamin said, "Yes."

The guard gave him nothing and started eating with relish to make it even worse for young Benjamin.

After lunch the guards changed, so Benjamin asked the new guard.

"I have to go to the bathroom."

The guard looked at his watch, and said, "I'll give you five minutes."

Benjamin went to the washroom. There was no bathroom. The washroom was nothing more than another barracks, a wooden barrack. It had two long ditches where you went for a bowel movement or to urinate. In the middle of the room there were two long pipes with faucets, ten or twenty faucets of cold water. The washroom was not guarded. It was always open.

Benjamin poured as much cold water on him as he could and was back in two minutes. Even though the guard gave him five minutes, Benjamin was back quickly because he was afraid of getting beat up again.

The concentration camps had only three punishments: Mental torture, physical abuse, and death. There were no other punishments.

Every block, every barrack had an SS officer who was responsible for that block. Benjamin was in block number five. The SS officer assigned to Benjamin's block was a very tall, slim, non-smiling, hard-nosed German. Since Benjamin committed this crime at the working site and Benjamin was a member of his block, the SS officer came to pay his respects.

He took Benjamin into the stubendienst, the office. The person in charge of the stubendienst was a privileged häftling, a prisoner. He was a French prisoner who was in a privileged position. All he had to do was take care of the barracks, count the people, and distribute the food. He was not hungry or thin. He lived in an office, and he had two youngsters to serve him. These two young boys stayed in his room, cleaned his room, and warmed his bed. He made homosexuals out of them, two boys Benjamin knew, who lived not far from Benjamin's hometown. They were two brothers, about Benjamin's age. Their chance of survival was good because the French häftling sheltered them. They never went out to work. They cleaned his room, made his bed, and engaged in sex acts with him.

In the afternoon this French häftling allowed Benjamin to go to the washroom. About four o'clock Benjamin's block was given their dinner. Dinner consisted of different things every day, mostly bread and a little something with what they called coffee.

Benjamin's raised his hand and asked, "Please, can I go to collect my supper."

He answered, "No."

Each time an SS officer came into the stubendienst, they would give Benjamin a kick or two just to let Benjamin know that they knew why he was there. The whole camp knew. The whole work detail was held up for two and a half hours. They came in and hit Benjamin all day long. When Benjamin was refused food by the French häftling, he knew he was going to be very hungry.

At six o'clock there was an *appel* when the roll call took place. They started lining up at 5:30 to make sure the prisoners were counted correctly and were in the correct place. Everybody had to stand in his own designated place.

The Lagerführer came in through the main gate. Benjamin was not far from him. Benjamin was standing at attention next to the gate, next to the barbed wires. If the Lagerführer had a special message, he would announce it. When he did not have any messages, he would step forward out of his car, and the lager accountant who was called the secretary would give the count. The lager accountant was a German prisoner, probably a communist or someone who did not support the Nazis. He had a privileged life. He was healthy. He ate well. He would report to the Lagerführer, he would raise his hand, and he would announce the accounting of the prisoners. He would say so many were here now on the *appel*, so many were at work outside the camp, so many were in the revier, which was the so-called clinic, and one was by the wire. Benjamin had to be included in the report.

CHAPTER 29

The Lagerführer, the head officer in charge of the camp can make all kinds of decisions. Benjamin knew his name once but has long since forgotten it. After the war when they needed some identification that Benjamin was in the camp, he had no identification. The man in charge of the office looked Benjamin up in the books by Benjamin's number in the Mauthausen book. Benjamin told him his number.

He said, "Okay, I find you here. I have your number. How do I know it is you who had that number?" Many others who were not camps used other people's names and numbers who had died to get this identity in order to be able to immigrate to America. Some Germans did it; some former Nazis did it.

"How do I know that you were in Mauthausen? I have your Mauthausen number. How do I know it is yours?" he asked.

"Okay, I will give you a test." He was a survivor of Mauthausen.

He asked Benjamin, "What camp in Mauthausen were you in?" Anybody who was not in Mauthausen could not answer that question.

Benjamin told him, "I was in camp number three."

"Where was camp number three in relation to one and two?" he asked.

Benjamin described it.

He then said, "Okay, now I know you were in Mauthausen. How do I know you were in Melk?"

So Benjamin described Melk to him.

Then he had a final question, "What was the name of the Lagerfuhrer in Melk?"

Benjamin said, "I knew the name but I forgot it."

He said, "All right, I'll give you five names, multiple choice, five names. If you can pick him out, we are done."

Benjamin told him. He knew the name; he had just forgotten it.

After the accounting was done, the Lagerführer turned towards Benjamin.

"Come here, come here," he said.

Benjamin moved toward the Lagerfuhrer. They did not let him get too close.

He said, "Warum wurden Sie schlafen?"[20]

He did not wait for an answer, bang with his right hand, and Benjamin fell down. The guys picked him up. Benjamin could not stand up by himself. The soldiers picked him up, and then he hit Benjamin on the other side. They picked Benjamin up again.

Benjamin was one of the few häftlings who had the distinguished honor to be addressed by the Lagerführer.

"You're going back to your barracks where you will get your meal and be ready to go out again at night shift, because you slept enough last night," said the Lagerführer . He also left orders at Benjamin's barrack that they should not exchange Benjamin with anybody else, even though Benjamin was in no condition to go out that night to work night shift because Benjamin could hardly walk.

The block eldester can make exchanges. If the Lagerführer had not given that direction, then the block eldester could have, if he wanted to, send somebody else in Benjamin's place. The Lagerführer made sure this would not happen. He gave his order. Then he dismissed everybody to go back to his barracks. Benjamin did not go back to the barracks. He went immediately to the washroom to wash up and drink some water. He had stood there in the heat from ten in the morning until six in the evening, eight hours.

---

[20] Why were you sleeping?

CHAPTER 30

While he was washing up, Benjamin heard an announcement made on the public address system.

"The one who slept this morning at the working site must report to his barracks immediately."

The Nazi block Führer was waiting for Benjamin. Each block had a German Nazi SS in charge. The SS was waiting for Benjamin because they expected Benjamin to go from the *appel* to the block, but he did not. He went to the washroom instead. So Benjamin came running. They took Benjamin into the block eldester's room, the office of this French prisoner. He took a chair and two people held Benjamin's hands, two people held Benjamin's legs. They bent Benjamin over the chair, and the SS block Führer took a rod of some kind and started hitting Benjamin. He hit Benjamin from the neck down as far as he could go and with force. Benjamin broke away from them in spite of his weakness. He could not take this pain. He broke away from them when they had counted to 30 or 32.

Then he said, "If you don't want the 50 I was going to mete out to you, I'll teach you a lesson."

Then he started hitting Benjamin with his fists, which was worse than the rod he was using. Benjamin was now bleeding from his mouth and his nose. The others just looked on. He then threw Benjamin out of the room right in front of the barracks, half dead.

As soon as the German SS Block Führer left, the French block eldester sent some boys to bring water from the washroom to bring Benjamin back to life. They poured water all over Benjamin. Then they carried Benjamin to his bed in block number five. Benjamin was too weak to walk. Doctor Adler who slept under Benjamin, borrowed towels and put wet towels around Benjamin's body. Benjamin's whole body was a wound.

They gave Benjamin something to eat, and then he went to sleep. They woke Benjamin up an hour later to go out on the night shift, and he went to the night shift. Benjamin had to be supported by two men, one on each side because he could not walk on his own. They put Benjamin on the train. When they arrived at the construction site, the prisoners lined up unit by unit depending on what your work assignment was.

Before the work began, the kapo, the person in charge of the shift shouted, "Where is the one who slept this morning?" The kapo was a Nazi, a German gypsy; he was in charge of that shift. He said, "You are being punished, we are not allowing you to be a spitzen traeger any more."

A spitzen traeger was an easy job. You could survive. Benjamin was no longer a spitzen traeger. Instead, Benjamin was sent to the machinist line. This job consisted of carrying machines out of the tunnel and into the tunnel on your shoulders. It took six to eight people to lift up the machinery and carry it. This was the hardest job there. If Benjamin had been given a chance to go back to the spitzen traeger job, he may have recovered, but sending him to the hardest job, Benjamin knew he would never make it out of the camp.

For about two weeks Benjamin stayed on that job. He could not to do much of the work, but he was assigned there. The other guys did the work. Then Benjamin was assigned to do some shoveling. The shovels were on a conveyor belt and Benjamin had to pick up a big shovel on the conveyor belt. The shovels were snow shovel size, and you had to make sure it was full of rocks. If the shovel was not full, you would be beaten. If nobody was watching, you would take it easy.

CHAPTER 31

After the beatings, Benjamin went through indescribable emotional anguish. Benjamin knew he was dying. His friend knew Benjamin was dying. Benjamin had a recurring nightmare. Benjamin dreamt that he was being beaten while he slept. Benjamin protested.

"You can't beat me while I'm asleep, this is my rest time. At work you can beat me, not here."

Benjamin screamed out a lot of things at night. Dr. Adler told him, as did others, that Benjamin was screaming at night.

Then one night while working alone, Benjamin saw the gypsy kapo coming toward him, and Benjamin started working faster.

"No, no, relax, put it down, put down the shovel," the gypsy kapo said.

Benjamin put down the shovel.

"Tell me something, how in the world did you expect to escape? How do you think you could make it?" he asked.

"I wasn't escaping. I was sleeping," Benjamin told him.

Then he started talking to Benjamin in a friendly way, asking about Benjamin's family, how Benjamin got to the camp, where Benjamin was born, and what Benjamin did as a child. After a few minutes of talking, the kapo walked away.

The following night Benjamin, thinking the kapo was sympathetic, lined up with the spitzen traegers. There were about twenty spitzen traegers. Benjamin thought, "What do I have to lose?"

Benjamin stood in the back of the line. The kapo stood in the front. He came over to the line and counted the spitzen traegers. The kapo saw Benjamin, gave Benjamin a mild smile, and allowed Benjamin to stay with the spitzen traegers. But for that act of kindness by that kapo, Benjamin would not have survived.

Once Benjamin got back to working as a spitzen traeger, he had new hope. Although Benjamin was very weak, slowly, he began to recover. He did not recover full health, nobody there had full health, nobody there was healthy, but Benjamin recovered. He was still alive. For seven to eight months, the whole winter and half of the spring, Benjamin continued to work as a spitzen traeger until he was liberated.

Benjamin saw his friend almost daily. Even when his friend was moved to another block, Benjamin could still see him any day, because after work they could get together. Life went on. The winter came. The prisoners lived like rats. In late fall or early winter, the prisoners were given overcoats. The overcoats were of the same striped material as the prison uniforms. It was not any thicker than the jackets, but it was longer. In the back of the coat they cut out a piece and put on a Star of David so that the German guards knew you were a Jewish prisoner. A star identified every prisoner. The red stars were for the criminals. The green stars were for political prisoners.

During that summer of 1944, there were planes flying over the camp, glittering silver planes, in formation, four, six, eight planes. Benjamin knew something was happening in Europe but did not know then about the Normandy Landing.

CHAPTER 32

By this time the German anti-air defense was zero. The planes could not be shot down. Nobody even tried to shoot them down. These planes flew over the camp on a daily basis, and at about the same time, around 11, 11:30 in the morning. The prisoners believed they were going to bomb Vienna or even Budapest.

One morning at about 11:20 a.m., the camp was bombed. There was a clock on one of the buildings. Melk was originally a military training camp for soldiers, and they lived in brick buildings, and one of the brick buildings had a little turret with a clock. When the Germans turned it into a concentration camp, they built a few dozen wooden barracks alongside the brick buildings.

When the bombarding took place, Benjamin was asleep because he had worked the night shift. He was asleep in the brick building on the second floor. The building had three floors. All of a sudden Benjamin was awakened by the sound of bombing and a distress signal. Benjamin woke up and jumped off his bed stepping on dead bodies. The planes were flying so low they were firing machine guns through the windows. They were not bombing or firing at the wooden barracks, only at the brick barracks. They probably did not think that there would be any prisoners in the brick barracks. Benjamin quickly ran out and hid in the ditches. The prisoners had made the ditches. Benjamin stayed in the ditches until the all-clear siren blew.

The bombs had broken some of the fences so a number of the prisoners tried to escape. Guards were firing from their posts. Some of the prisoners managed to escape. But once outside, it was not easy. If you sheltered a prisoner, you would be shot. What Benjamin did know was there were several hundred guys missing. Whether they were killed or escaped, only the Germans knew.

When the winter came, the prisoners slept in unheated barracks. It was very cold in Austria with a great deal of snow.

Although the winter coat was very light, it was an extra covering, an extra layer of clothing. In addition to this prison issued coat, there were also some civilian overcoats that were given to some of the prisoners, mostly to the younger prisoners. These civilian overcoats probably came from Auschwitz or other places were Jews had been exterminated and their clothing confiscated. The idea was to give the coats to the youth and give them a better chance to survive. Benjamin was very happy with that coat. Not only did he use it when he went to work, but he also used it as an extra blanket at night to keep himself warm. Benjamin had the coat for about a month. Then someone stole it at night while Benjamin was sleeping. That was the end of the warm overcoat. The rest of the winter Benjamin had to manage with the thin prison coat.

Before the winter when the Jewish holidays came, Rosh Hashanah, and Yom Kippur, some of the prisoners got together after work to have a prayer service on Rosh Hashanah at night with no book. There were some Jews there who were learned and knew the prayers by heart. Benjamin knew most of them by heart. Here they were at midnight in this valley of tears, in this valley of blood, praying together to celebrate the New Year. The tears were flowing while the prisoners chanted and sang those beautiful Rosh Hashanah hymns and prayers and melodies.

CHAPTER 33

On Rosh Hashanah 1944, during the *appel*, the Lagerführer wished the Jewish members a happy new year. "I wish you a Happy New Year, and I hope that in this year you will be reunited with your families."

Some people thought he was being sarcastic. Benjamin did not. Benjamin thought he meant it. To be reunited with your loved ones could mean reunited in heaven. That is where most of them were, but Benjamin did not think he meant it that way. In the winter of 1944 the food improved dramatically. The prisoners were given double bread rations. In the morning where they used to get an eighth of a loaf of bread, they were given a quarter. Sometimes you were given double rations in the morning and double rations in the evening. The soups improved. They were also given some kind of a macaroni and milk, unheard of in a concentration camp.

For a while, the prisoners were given cigarettes, even for the teenagers. Once a week the prisoners were given a small package of ten cigarettes, manufactured in Czechoslovakia by the name of Zory. Benjamin did not smoke, so he traded his cigarettes for food. The heavy smokers were willing to give up a little of their food in order to be able to smoke. The Lagerführer was responsible for these improvements.

The prisoners worked for a private firm. The German government hired them out. The prisoners were leased out to private firms for so much per day per worker. The Lagerführer negotiated with the private firms.

He told the factory owners, "They are working too hard. You must feed them better."

The Lagerführer was not a typical SS officer. He was not, a typical sadistic or brutal man. At the end of the war, he got a light sentence because some ex-Melk inmates testified favorably. He got five years instead of twenty-five or thirty. So when he wished them a Happy New Year, Benjamin felt he meant it.

The food improved dramatically to the extent that no one at Melk died of starvation. The prisoners were always hungry, but no one died of starvation. Benjamin, along with the other teenagers, would get their meals at the construction site. They would bring about a half dozen huge cast iron steel containers with soup or potatoes. The chief kapo would distribute the food for about twenty-five hundred people. He had to be very careful. It had to be enough for everybody. He would give small portions to make sure that the last people would get their share. As a result, he usually had leftovers. When he had leftovers, he would give the teenagers a second helping. Although this German kapo was brutal to the adults, he was kinder to the children. He was terribly brutal to the Russians. At the end of the war, after they were liberated, the Russians caught and killed him with their own hands. They just tore him apart.

On Yom Kippur, Benjamin was on the 3 p.m. to 11 p.m. afternoon shift. Benjamin had his dinner in the afternoon at the construction site, and then he fasted. Some of the prisoners fasted, no food, no drink, and then went to work that night. When Benjamin came back from work, he celebrated Kol Nidre night around midnight. The morning bread that he was given he took with him, not to be eaten until the fast was over. Benjamin worked two shifts on Kol Nidre, on Yom Kippur day, one during the night, one during the day. Two shifts without food. He did not eat, and God would have forgiven Benjamin even if he had, just as God would forgive Benjamin for eating non-kosher food to stay alive.

For survival you are allowed to eat anything. The Torah says you should live through the Torah, not die. In other words, if your life is in danger you can set aside most of the Torah. You can set aside the Torah if your life is in danger, except in three instances. For these three you must observe the Torah even if your life is in danger.

The first is murder. If somebody orders you to murder somebody you cannot do it, even though somebody threatens to kill you. Murder is not excusable under any circumstances.

The second is incest. You cannot engage in incest, even if it costs you your life.

The third is denying your God, denying your religion, which in many instances the prisoners were forced to do. Some could not withstand the pressure and converted.   Others said no, and they suffered death.

CHAPTER 34

The winter was a very, very hard winter, snow, rain mixed with snow, sleet. Benjamin and the other prisoners were practically naked against this weather. The little thin things they wore provided little warmth or comfort. They were also seriously undernourished and hungry all the time. This decreased their resistance to diseases.

Benjamin recalled one special day when the prisoners stood on the ramp outside Melk to be taken to the construction site. It was late November or early December 1944. The train did not come at its usual time. It had other priorities. Military trains had priorities. The prisoners stood there for about an hour and a half waiting for the train with heavy wet snow soaking them. Many people died from that weather. Benjamin survived.

Walking down from the camp to the platform where the train ramp was about a thirty-minute walk. As the prisoners marched to the train, there were Germans on each side with rifles pointing at the prisoners. There was little space between the guards, and the prisoners walked slowly. Normally, the train came soon after they arrived at the platform, but not this day. Everybody was sick that night.

The construction site was about eight minutes away by train. From Melk to the construction site, the train went through a tunnel. Each train car had two armed guards. The doors of the train were kept open. There was one door on each side of the train in the middle.

One day Benjamin was seated against the wall on the right side. Before the train moved, the guard called Benjamin over.

He said, "I want you to sit up front, not there." While they went through the tunnel and the other guard could not see anything, he gave Benjamin a piece of bread. Here, was an SS guard giving Benjamin a piece of bread. He had collected it from his own mess hall. He had to wait until the train was in the tunnel. Otherwise, the other guard would have reported him. Giving bread to a Jew. This was a crime. This illustrates that not every German was a beast.   Some of them still had human kindness in them.

There were no women at the camp. Benjamin had not seen a woman's face since arriving at the camps. One day while waiting for the train in a heavy snow, a train came by and stopped right in front of Benjamin carrying a train full of young German women all dressed up going east to serve the soldiers. The prisoners had no contact with women.

CHAPTER 35

The Russian soldiers sang some songs from time to time. Benjamin did not remember anyone else singing songs. In Melk you were in hell.

The Jewish prisoners did not celebrate the Sabbath. One day Benjamin spotted a middle-aged man working on some piece of machinery. He called Benjamin over to talk him. They talked in Yiddish.

"Where are you from? Who is your father?" he asked

Benjamin told him. He knew Benjamin's father.

"What Yeshiva did you study in? What part of the Talmud did you study?" he asked.

Benjamin told him, and they started studying the Talmud together, just the two of them alone in this tunnel. Benjamin had forgotten some of it, but the man helped Benjamin. They went over the melody with the intonations of the Talmud. They studied together for about half an hour in this hell called Melk, a rabbi from Hungary and a Jewish boy from Hungary.

The angels in heaven must have rejoiced. Look at the deep mess they are in, but they are studying Talmud. The angels must have said, "People like this deserve to be saved."

Benjamin found out a week or two later who the man was and what town he was from. He did not tell Benjamin that he was the rabbi from a town and ran the Yeshiva there. His town was about fifty kilometers from Benjamin's town. He survived. After the war this rabbi had a place in Borough Park, Brooklyn, New York. Benjamin went there once after the war. When the services were over, Benjamin went over to talk to him.

"Good shabbas rabbi," Benjamin said. "Rabbi, I have to tell you something. You were with me in Melk, and you studied *Gmoro* with me. You studied *Gmoro* with me in the camp."

And the rabbi said, "I remember." Who could forget?

It is important to know about the lack of cleanliness in the camp. Nobody had more than one shirt, one pair of pants, one jacket, or one cap. Nobody had underwear. No one had much of a chance to wash his clothes. In the summertime, they might go to the washroom after coming home from the morning shift and wash the shirt with cold water. The shirt would dry on your shoulders if you went out. You could not wash the shirt in the winter. Benjamin wore his shirt for about six months without washing it. After his severe beating, Benjamin had a severe wound on his back under his shoulder. Benjamin carried that scar the rest of his life. Benjamin did not go to the clinic for treatment because he was afraid. Once you went to the clinic, it was hard to get out. Most people went from the clinic to cremation.

Benjamin treated the wound himself by putting margarine on it. This made it worse. It became infected with pus. It would stick to his shirt. The whole winter this process went on. Benjamin's wound was full of pus. It would dry and stick to his shirt. Then it would tear away. Benjamin had the same shirt until the end of the war.

In the middle of the night if you had to go to the bathroom—if you just had to relieve yourself of water—there was a big bucket in front of the block. But if you had to go to move your bowels, you could not do that in the block. You had to go out in the ice-cold weather with your light clothing in the middle of the night. You had to go out to a separate place. The campsite was guarded all night. There were kapos all around. The camp was not wholly asleep. So Benjamin would run out barefoot in the cold to go to the bathroom.

The kapo would ask, "Who are you?"

The kapo had to make sure that Benjamin was not trying to escape.

Lice were a big problem. There were all kinds of lice. They grew on your body and in your clothing. Benjamin was full of lice. He would feel something itchy, would scratch it, and lice would come out. Lice carried diseases. Many people died of typhus. Living or dying, prisoners were never examined by a doctor. When they died, they were just cremated.

One night in the winter of 1945, the lice were so terrible that Benjamin could not fall asleep. He did not sleep the whole night, and he had to go to work the next day. Every few weeks the prisoners were given a shower. They would be taken block by block. There were too many prisoners to shower at the same time. Benjamin got about six or seven showers for the entire year.

During the time that you were showering, your clothing was disinfected. Each piece of clothing had your numbers on it so it could not be interchanged with someone else's clothes. This disinfection process was supposed to kill the lice, but it did not. Two days later you had lice again but a little less than before. That was the extent of the hygiene.

Nobody brushed his teeth. There was hardly any soap to wash. In Melk you could not escape. There were too many guards. Even if you could manage to escape from the guards, you had on this concentration camp uniform. If anybody saw you they would know who you were and would report you. One Russian boy did escape, probably by stealing

CHAPTER 36

To make it even more difficult to escape, the prisoners' hair was shaved with a two-inch stripe down the middle. The barbers would come every week and wake the prisoners when they were asleep. They had barbers coming and going from barracks to barracks with razors. They did not sharpen the razors every day. It was very painful, but you had to endure it. People died all over the place. People died at work. People died in the barracks. People died in the clinic.

Benjamin saw people die. He saw people being shot just before liberation. Early in the winter of 1944 there were rumors that the war was going very badly for the Germans. The war was not going to last very much longer. If liberation was coming, Benjamin did not want to die the day before the liberation.

One day in March of 1945, during roll call, the Lagerführer announced, "There will no longer be any work."

In fact, a group of soldiers did go out to the construction site and blew it up. The Germans did not want the incoming armies to find these tunnels.

The Lagerführer told the prisoners that the front was coming closer and that it would be dangerous. To protect the prisoners he would be evacuating the camp. He would be moving them further away from the Russians and the Americans. The Russians were moving west. The Americans were moving east. Eventually they would meet up. This was a terrible blow to the prisoners. The prisoners wanted to stay there because the Russians were a couple of days away at that time, and they would have been liberated.

The Lagerführer evacuated the whole camp, not just Jews, but the entire camp. During that *appel,* he offered those who felt they could not walk transportation by train. Most of the prisoners did not trust him. They thought if you were too weak to walk that you would be killed. People were afraid to admit that they were too weak to walk, and they did not ask to go by train. Benjamin did ask, and he was right. A train was provided. The train took a few hundred prisoners back to Mauthausen, the mother camp. Benjamin did not know what happened to the other prisoners until after the war. Mauthausen was so crowded that everyone slept on the floor. They were packed in like sardines.

The kapo said, "You lay here, next person the other way around, head one way and head the other way."

They were given very little food to eat. Mauthausen had three camps. Benjamin was in camp three. In the corner Benjamin found a heap of coals, and he ate some coals. Benjamin was very hungry. He heard that the Germans made margarine from coals, so he thought it would be good to eat. Benjamin stuffed himself with coals to get a little bit of nourishment. Nobody else did it. Benjamin's friends would not touch it. This was about ten days before the end of the war. During those ten days Benjamin had no bowel movement.

PART THREE

"When I despair, I remember that all through history the way of truth and love have always won. There have been tyrants and murderers, and for a time, they can seem invincible, but in the end, they always fall. Think of it--always."

Mahatma Gandhi

CHAPTER 37

In Melk and in Mauthausen, there was no religious discrimination. All prisoners, Jews and non-Jews, were treated the same. However, when Benjamin returned to Mauthausen after the evacuation, all the Jews were moved out of the camp. Outside the camp, tents were set up for the Jewish prisoners. The Jews were no longer treated like officially registered prisoners. They were left alone. There was no more counting, no more roll calls. The little food they received consisted of a loaf of brick shaped bread. The bread appeared to be very old, maybe it came from the first world war. There was green mold inside. The bread was shared by eight people, and they were given a drink they called coffee, which was not coffee. There was no more work. They stayed there for about a week. The tents were guarded. About twenty people could sleep in a tent. You would sleep wherever you could find a place to sleep. Not only were there Jews from the main camp of Mauthausen, there were a large number of Hungarian Jews who were never in a concentration camp.

These Hungarian Jews had towels and linen and their own regular clothing with coats. In one of those tents there were two people from Solotvyno, Benjamin's hometown. One was a boy a couple of years younger than Benjamin. He was a dentist's son. The other was a friend of Benjamin's father. He was a top scholar in Judaica. He wrote books. He lectured. He was a little younger than Benjamin's father. If he were not young, he would not have been in the labor force. Only those younger than forty-two were in the labor force. He was a very wealthy man. He made a lot of money after the war and built a Yeshiva in his name in Israel. He and his wife survived.

They were kept in those tents for a few days and then they were to be evacuated because the Russians were closing in on Mauthausen. The Germans did not want any Jews to be freed. That was an order from Himmler. No Jews should be allowed to be liberated to give testimony to what happened. Did he think he could hide this from the world? Eventually, the world would know.

The non-Jews were left in the camps to be liberated. The Jews were evacuated and forced to march with little food. They were given a little brown soup once a day with no bread. For many this was a death march. They would march in groups of hundreds. Hundreds and hundreds would be separated because they were separately guarded. They would walk for an hour or so and then be allowed to rest a little on the side of the road. After a short rest they were ordered to get up and walk. Some people could not get up or did not want to get up. They wanted to die.

The guard would ask, "Are you coming or are you staying?"

The prisoner would say, "I'm staying, shoot me." And the guard would shoot the prisoner. No living person was left behind. Benjamin heard plenty of shots. The sides of the road were lined with those people who did not want to live any more. They did not want to be liberated either. What kind of world was out there beyond liberation? They were going to be liberated into a world that created the conditions inside the camp.

They had family before. They had a family of three or four children, and they knew that they were all dead. So a prisoner would say, "What am I going to be liberated to? Go back to? The anti-Semitic world? Back to Hungary? Back to Germany? I don't want that."

Benjamin fell behind because he could not keep up. He would keep moving back in the lines of hundreds. By the end of the march, Benjamin was in the last two groups. They went through a town marching. One night they slept in the fields. Guards surrounded them. They were told not to get up at night.

"If you get up at night, we will consider that that you are attempting to escape, and we will shoot you. Stay down until we wake you," the guard said.

Benjamin remembers being marched through a town called Wels. They saw a woman, a young Austrian woman, nicely dressed, come out with a bag of groceries from a grocery store, and the prisoners attacked her for her food. The Germans tried to push the prisoners with their guns to go back to the line, but it did not help. The prisoners did not care they were so hungry. The prisoners were also fighting each other for the food. Benjamin was able to grab a few mushrooms to eat. After leaving Wels, the prisoners walked for about an hour and then were given a rest period. During that rest period, Benjamin was so hungry that he ate some daisies and dandelions. Benjamin had no way of knowing whether what he was eating was safe to eat, but he was so hungry he did not care. He ate this greenery because it was spring. He ate from the gutter. He found snails in a dirty gutter and sucked out the snail from its shell just like you would suck out an egg from its shell. He ate about two or three snails. It was nourishment and might keep him going for another day. Others also ate snails and flowers and grass.

CHAPTER 38

The prisoners were forced to march again for another hour or so, and then they were ordered to stop. There was a forest to the left of the prisoners, and they were ordered into the forest. Benjamin was sure they were going to be killed in the forest. When men with guns order you to go to the forest, you go to the forest. There was no road. There was just some narrow passage there. Deep in the forest there was a camp. The town near this forest was called Gunskirchen. It means "Blessed Church." The prisoners were not taken to the town of Gunskirchen. They were taken to the forest. It was a Saturday morning when they marched into that forest and into the camp. There were very heavy rains all day, and the prisoners were soaked. The prisoners had left Mauthausen on Wednesday and arrived in this camp on Saturday. Trees were cut down to make a camp that could not be seen from the outside.

The prisoners were horrified, even those who had seen the worst, were horrified. The camp was all muddy from the rain. Outside each wooden barrack there were heaps of corpses. They no longer buried them. They no longer cremated them. A few of the prisoners who died during the night or during the day were piled on top of the dead corpses. Each barrack had a pile of corpses. Some of the prisoners were eating the corpses. In the last days of the war, there was cannibalism.

There were no words to describe the horrors Benjamin and the other prisoners suffered. Could hell be worse than this? The world will never know the details. A person who was not there would find the horrors incomprehensible.

Gunskirchen was not a camp in the normal sense. Gunskirchen was an open grave: a place where they brought the prisoners to die. Benjamin did not know how many thousands of dead were in this open grave. The barracks had no floor. There were no bunks. There was no straw used for mattresses. In Melk the barracks had bunks, and each bunk had a little straw even for a mattress. You were counted each time, and you had a chance to wash. You went to work. You socialized.

At Gunskirchen you came to die. You were brought there to die or to survive if you could survive. The prisoners were not registered. They were not counted. They were fed molded bread to be distributed between eight or ten people.

The total population of Gunskirchen at that time was between three thousand and four thousand people.

There were about eight barracks in the camp. In front of each barrack there was a pile of bodies, naked, very emaciated bodies. Mostly skin and bones with terrible faces. Nobody even bothered to close his or her eyes.

The first night Benjamin slept in one of the barracks on the muddy floor because it was raining all that week. The next morning when Benjamin woke up, the person next to him was dead. It was no big deal. They picked him up and added him to the pile outside. That was his funeral.

The next night, Benjamin did not want to sleep in the barracks. He slept outside. It was already the end of April, beginning of May, and it was warm enough to sleep outside. Many others slept outside. You slept with the dying and the dead.

On Tuesday, there were rumors that the prisoners were going to get food from the Red Cross. Parcels were sent to the camps all through the war, except the prisoners never saw any of this food. The Germans ate those Red Cross parcels meant for the prisoners. On Wednesday morning, there was an announcement that teenagers should line up in front of this barrack for food from the Red Cross. It was the first time that Benjamin even heard the word "Red Cross" in a camp. People from the Red Cross never saw or visited the prisoners.

CHAPTER 39

In this population of several thousand dying people, only teenagers were supposed to line up to get this food. Everybody was a teenager now, twenty year olds, twenty-five year olds, and older men pushed into the line. There were Germans with rifles that weeded out the older prisoners. The Germans would push them out of the line and hit them with their rifles.

While Benjamin was standing in line, there was a little commotion because some guys were not supposed to be in the line. The Germans had a little battle going on with them, and Benjamin was standing there. A German soldier hit Benjamin with the butt of his gun straight in Benjamin's lower back spine. Benjamin could not get up. Benjamin could not breathe deeply. If he did, he felt pain in his lower back. When he coughed, he felt pain. There was nobody to take care of him. There was no doctor to go to. This was Wednesday. There was an announcement over the public address system, the first time that Benjamin was allowed to listen to the radio. Never before did Benjamin get any report or news of the progress or lack of progress of the German armies. The collapse of the German army was imminent and the liberation of the camp was also imminent. The only question was who would still be alive.

On Thursday the camp commandant announced that he was looking for prisoners who could speak English. The camp commandant took a couple of translators with him in his car with a white flag to meet the American army. He was surrendering the camp to the Americans. He showed the Americans an order he received to kill everybody in the camp, and that no one should remain alive. He told them he did not follow this order.

On Friday, May 8, Benjamin knew it was the day of liberation. The guards who had been there all week were gone. Prisoners were coming with breads. Some prisoners were carrying guns. Benjamin was free. He did not wait for the Americans. Benjamin and a group of youngsters found an opening in the fence and went through this opening to look for food, for shelter, for clean clothing. There were four or five youngsters with Benjamin heading in the same direction.

The first thing they saw when they got past the fence was an American woman, a military officer on a horse. She was holding her gun in the ready position but not toward Benjamin. The Americans had to clear out individual Germans, who were still shooting at them. Benjamin started screaming. What if this woman did not know they were prisoners? She was coming towards Benjamin and the other youngsters with a gun ready to fire, and they were screaming.

She said, "No, no, don't be afraid." She spoke in English. No one understood her. Then she left and continued her own mission.

A little later they came to a farm and saw an American soldier kissing and necking with a blonde German girl. Benjamin and the other boys were all disgusted. How could he kiss a German girl? She was the enemy.

They came to a farmhouse. At the farmhouse, they saw German kitchen kettles. In those kettles there was macaroni soup with milk, rich, clean. It was delicious, and it was still warm. They ate their fill. This farm was about twenty minutes from the camp. The food was in a separate building just outside the farm. After they finished eating they went into the farmhouse. In the farmhouse there were prisoners from the camp. There was no food left on the table, and they already assigned who was going to sleep in the beds and the building. Benjamin was told there was no room left, and he and the boys with him could sleep in the barn on hay.

The German family members were around the table serving the prisoners. One of the girls, a German blonde said, "I have something I can still give you."

She went and got some food preserves and told them they could sleep in the barn on the hay. There were about four or five of teenagers sleeping on the hay. They considered themselves liberated although they had not seen the liberator.

They got up that next morning realizing that they were now free. It took a while for this to sink in. For the past year Benjamin's tormentors ordered every movement Benjamin made. Now the tormentors were gone. Benjamin had to think for himself. The boys broke into groups of two going from house to house.   Then Benjamin was alone going from house to house looking for food.   The first day after the first night the Germans were glad to give the former prisoners food.   There was plenty of food, and Benjamin could not stop eating.

CHAPTER 40

Liberation was Friday. On Monday Benjamin came out to a main road and saw black American soldiers driving jeeps. Benjamin had never seen a black person. At first he thought that all Americans were black. They seemed so powerful driving around in those jeeps with guns. They were there to pick up the prisoners who had escaped the camps. They wanted to check out the prisoners for medical reasons. The prisoners had many diseases that could be spread. Benjamin did his best to evade the Americans. One night Benjamin slept in a train that was filled with food. But, Benjamin's back pain was so severe, he decided it was time to go back to the camp and have his back checked out medically. So when he saw a jeep, instead of trying to avoid it, he allowed himself to be picked up and brought back to the camp.

When Benjamin came back to the camp, he saw the soldiers carrying many of the former prisoners to makeshift clinics. Many of these people were half dead. When Benjamin arrived, he was taken on a truck to one of the makeshift clinics. An American doctor examined him. After examining Benjamin the doctor found that Benjamin was too healthy to be admitted to the clinic. When Benjamin pointed to his back, the doctor said it was not broken and that Benjamin would be fine. Benjamin came back the next day and insisted that he be reexamined. They took an x-ray that showed Benjamin back was not broken, but was badly bruised. They admitted Benjamin into the clinic. There were eight people to a room. The doctors who were treating the patients were German doctors, and no one trusted them. Yesterday, they were the enemy. Today, they were the healers. Benjamin had no choice.

While being treated at the clinic, Benjamin met someone from his hometown. Benjamin had no way of knowing that he was also at the camp in Gunskirchen. People were brought there from many places. They were brought to Gunskirchen to die. He was a couple of years older than Benjamin, but he was gravely ill. He had a kidney infection and died several days later. Benjamin remembered the exact date because in later years his family members heard that Benjamin was in the same room with him when he died, and they wanted to establish the date in order to be able to observe the anniversary of his death. Benjamin told them.

Benjamin stayed at the clinic for six weeks. Very slowly, he was brought back to health. They were given no solid food, not even bread, because they could not hold it. They were given hot cereals and soups. Benjamin and the group he was with were the last ones to be liberated on the very last day of the war, May 8, 1945. Other camps had been liberated weeks before, so they had some experience what to do with these emaciated people, and then after a while they gave Benjamin some regular food. Very slowly he gained back his strength.

On his third week at the clinic, the doctor in charge of the medical staff looked at Benjamin's eyes and ordered a blood transfusion. They came in with a large flask of red blood. The nurses and doctors tried to find a vein where they could put the blood in, but Benjamin's veins were so dry, they could not find one. Doctor after doctor looked for a vein and could not find one to feed in the blood. Finally, the doctor who prescribed the blood transfusion came in and managed to find a vein. Benjamin fell asleep. When he woke up, the entire flask was empty. Liters and liters of blood. That helped Benjamin a great deal.

After about six weeks at the clinic, one of Benjamin's cousins from Benjamin's hometown who lived next door to Benjamin, and who had survived Auschwitz and Buchenwald and a few other camps, came to the window. He heard that Benjamin was there. They would not allow him into the clinic so he came to the window of Benjamin's room. Benjamin ran to the window, and there was Benjamin's first cousin, Simcha. Simcha is a Hebrew word meaning joy or gladness.

After the war, Simcha moved to Los Angeles. Benjamin visited him quite frequently. Benjamin stayed very close to him, and he to Benjamin. He was Benjamin's father's brother's son, something left from his father. Benjamin had other cousins who lived in Canada, but he did not speak to any of them after the war.

CHAPTER 41

Shortly after that, the Czechoslovakian government asked that its residents—its citizens who were in hospitals in the liberated lands, should be handed over to them. They would continue with the care-taking. They wanted to take over the care-taking of their own citizens.

So Benjamin and other Czech nationals were taken in a truck to another town there at the River Danube and put on a boat that took them back to Melk. They took Benjamin back to the camp where he was a slave for almost a year. The small boat held about a hundred people. They turned Melk into a facility for the liberated. It was hard to believe that Benjamin was a free person in the same place where he was never free. But he stayed in Melk only one night. Then he was taken by truck to Wiener Neustadt, which means New Vienna. From Wiener Neustadt Benjamin was taken to Prague. There were special buildings assigned for camp returnees where they were given food. They were also sent to a place where they were deloused, disinfected with DDT. They sprayed it into your body and into your clothing. It did not go away for a long time.

In Prague they also took Benjamin to a building where there were rooms full of clothing that American families had donated for the survivors.

Benjamin stayed in Prague for a couple of weeks. He could hardly speak Czech any more, not having spoken it for over six years. Benjamin then headed to Budapest, Hungary, the country where he was living in before deportation. On the way to Budapest, the train made a stop in Bratislava, previously known as Pressburg. The Germans called it Pressburg. It was the second largest city in Czechoslovakia. It is now the capital of independent Slovakia. Bratislava used to be a very well established old Jewish community with a very scholarly Rabbi Schreiber, who had a yeshiva there in the late 17th century. There were kitchens set up and places to sleep. There was a kosher kitchen and a non-kosher kitchen. Benjamin went to the kosher kitchen by instinct. Benjamin ate well. They had very good food there, stews, soups, breads, cakes, anything you could imagine. After dinner Benjamin went to the non-kosher kitchen and ate some more.

While Benjamin was there, Benjamin met a young boy of thirteen or fourteen from Benjamin's hometown. He was the son of the only dentist in Solotvyno.

He asked Benjamin, "Did you see your brother?"

Benjamin asked, "No, where did you see my brother?"

He said, "He's in the next room."

That is how Benjamin met his older brother after the war. He was hard to recognize. His hair was shaven, and he had some kind of a funny cap, but there he was. They hugged, kissed, and cried, and were together again.

They stayed one more day in Pressburg and then headed towards Budapest to look for other possible survivors of their family. People were going to these larger cities where survivors were registered. Shortly after arriving in Budapest Benjamin's brother got very sick and was hospitalized. Benjamin was not sure what the problem was. He thought it might have been a heart problem. Benjamin stayed in Budapest and visited his brother every day bringing him some fresh fruits. They lived in a house that the Jewish organizations had set aside for them. They had no beds. They slept on the floor. They were happy. They were free. They slept.

CHAPTER 42

Benjamin talked with his brother about other family survivors. Nobody younger than Benjamin survived. All Benjamin's siblings were with him, and they were all sent to the left and instant death. But they had two older sisters, Leah and Miriam. Maybe they survived. Benjamin went back to Prague, back to Bratislava because the Czech survivors were coming there. Benjamin went back there a couple of times but could not find his sisters.

Benjamin would find people from his hometown and ask, "Did you see my sisters?"

Benjamin could not find his sisters. Many weeks later, Miriam, the younger of the two, did show up. Her last camp was Bergen-Belsen, which was liberated by the British. She had been hospitalized there for a long period with some serious disease. When she felt better she was let go, and she reunited with her surviving brothers in Budapest.

Before Miriam came from Bergen-Belsen, Benjamin learned that his other sister, Leah, had survived the war by staying in Budapest. She never left Budapest. She was not deported. She had false papers that listed her was as a gentile girl. This was very dangerous because she did not speak Hungarian like a native. If someone who had an ear for language, asked her about the town she was from, he would have known that she was not born there.

Benjamin heard that she had survived, was no longer in Budapest, had a boyfriend, and was on her way to Palestine. Benjamin knew very little about Palestine. In the Hasidic schools they did not teach you about modern day Palestine. They taught you only about ancient Israel when it was in Jewish hands, when the temple was there. It was a Jewish monarchy. Benjamin did not know that Jews were living in Palestine. He thought that all the Jews were driven out of Palestine. Benjamin found out later that there were Zionist organizations that were very active in recruiting survivors to resettle in Palestine.

Leah came back to Budapest a few weeks later to find out if any of her siblings had survived. That is why she came back. She was like a cold fish, no hugging, no kissing, no welcoming. She was with her boyfriend. She never expressed in words or in emotions that she was happy that her brothers survived. Instead of staying with her brothers, she went to Graz, Austria where the Zionists set up a camp for people to transport them to Palestine. She took Miriam with her, leaving her two younger brothers to fend for themselves. One brother was in the hospital. Yet, she left them without a forwarding address. Where would they find each other in the future? She left. She did not seem to care what happened to her two younger brothers. Benjamin was very troubled by his sister's uncaring attitude. Benjamin was the youngest survivor in his family, and his sisters left her two younger brothers without any plans for a future reunion. Benjamin was left with his older brother, who was still in a hospital in Budapest. Benjamin's two older sisters vanished. Where would they go? What would they do? They had no home to go back to.

Many other survivors had reasons to go back. There were people who had hid some of their money or jewelry hoping that the population of the village that went back did not uncover it. Well, they either found it or did not find it. Benjamin had no reason. Their parents had not buried any jewelry or money.

They instead went to Bratislava. They spent several weeks in Bratislava for Rosh Hashanah and Yom Kippur. Finally, they realized they had to go somewhere. They heard about the Displaced Persons camps in Germany and Austria. These camps were mostly, but not exclusively, Jewish camps. The United Nations Relief Association provided the funding for these camps. There were also Russian soldiers, who had survived the war, in these camps.

Benjamin heard that one of the camps had established a yeshiva, and that is where they went. The camp was close to Munich in a small town called Wolfratshausen. The camp itself was called Fernwald. Fernwald was a large camp with good housing units. They would keep you there until you emigrated somewhere. When Benjamin arrived in Fernwald with his older brother, both of their sisters were there. By this time, his older sister Leah had married her boyfriend. Leah's new husband was from Benjamin's hometown. He lived five or six houses away from Benjamin. Benjamin knew him from there. He had been married before with children. He lost his entire family.

Benjamin opposed the marriage very much. He had no reason to, but he did. He was a fine gentleman. He was a professional carpenter in town, maybe the only one. He was religious but not educated. In Benjamin's opinion he was not good enough for his sister. Benjamin cried about it. This brother-in-law never forgave Benjamin for that. Later, he caused Benjamin troubles and anguish.

He would always comment, "Remember, you cried because you didn't want me for your sister."

Benjamin was seventeen years old and had just been liberated. He cried. Benjamin had turned seventeen after the war in Wiener Neustadt, in the New Vienna on Benjamin's way to Prague.

What was left of the family was now together in Fernwald. Leah was now married and cooked for all of them. They ate together. But, they would soon part and go their separate ways.

CHAPTER 43

Britain had closed entrance to Palestine, and America was not giving visas to displaced persons, except to direct family members. A father could bring his daughters, but not distant relatives. President Truman made a statement in 1946 that the British should open Palestine for 100,000 of the survivors, but the British refused.

Benjamin learned that teenagers who had lost both their mother and father were being transported to England. Benjamin's brother was eighteen and could not go. Benjamin left his brother and two sisters to go on this transport. A transport of one hundred youngsters from Benjamin's hometown area was being transported, and Benjamin decided to go. He went on the train with a Polish fellow who was the same age as Benjamin. They had to take a train in the direction of the Czech border. There were no trains that went directly from Germany to Prague. There were no airlines. There were no buses. Germany was cut off. You had to go to the border and cross the border by foot and then take a train to Prague. Benjamin and his friend took a train to the actual border crossing, and when they arrived there, they were arrested at the border by United States military. They were taken to a small room and questioned by an American officer, but they did not know a word of English. Benjamin was searched, and they found four or five letters in Benjamin's pocket. It was illegal to carry mail, but Benjamin did not know that. Before Benjamin left the camp, some people had given Benjamin letters to mail to their American relatives. There was no mail going out from Germany. The only way you could mail letters was to take them to another country and then mail them from there where they could be mailed to America.

Benjamin was sentenced for a week in detention in a room. His friend did not have any letters and was not arrested, but he stayed with Benjamin to keep Benjamin company. Benjamin sent word to his brother and sisters that he was in detention, and Benjamin's brother came to visit him. When Benjamin was let go, he left with his friend to cross the border.   There were no passenger trains, so they got on a freight train and hid themselves. They made it to Plzen, a famous beer-making town, and were discovered and removed from the train by a Czech train employee. Benjamin was able to speak a little Czech and was able to explain that he was a national coming back from the camps. Benjamin's friend could not speak a word of Czech. He was Polish, so they played the game pretending he had a toothache and could not talk. Benjamin did the talking for both of them, and they were let go at about 2:00 or 3:00 a.m. They arrived in Prague and went to one of the houses where survivors were given free food to eat and free places to sleep. They then went to the Jewish neighborhood in Prague where an organization was there arranging a transport to England.

Benjamin had no legal documents showing where he was born. Fortunately, there were people there who could question Benjamin and determine that Benjamin was from where he said he was from. Benjamin was able to answer all the questions. Who was the rabbi of the village? Where did the rabbi live? Where was the synagogue? How many synagogues were there in the village? Who was the shochet? Where did he live? Benjamin answered all the questions and was released.

Benjamin found someone there from Solotvina. Benjamin knew him well. Both families knew each other. Benjamin spoke to him and learned that he had been educated in Prague before the German occupation in 1938. Benjamin told him that he wanted to get on the transport. Benjamin now had a firsthand witness, a live witness who knew Benjamin. That is how Benjamin was able get on the transport to England. Benjamin later learned when he came to New York that this friend made it to America and had a small business in Philadelphia.

Benjamin was put on a special train from Prague to Paris, stayed in a youth hostel in Giverny for three weeks, and then went by ship to London. There were about a hundred boys and girls on the train. They were all supposed to be orphans and under eighteen but there were some older than eighteen and some who had one parent still alive.

CHAPTER 44

When Benjamin arrived at the youth hostel in Giverny, he met Eli Wiesel. Eli Wiesel was from Sighet a town next to Benjamin's hometown, just across the river. Benjamin met Eli Wiesel again later when Benjamin came to Boston and Eli Wiesel was a professor at Boston University. The reason given for the three-week delay was that the facilities in London were not yet completed.

Benjamin was very well fed, housed, and entertained at the youth hostel. Benjamin was taken to Paris to see the sights. On one Sunday Benjamin was taken on a sightseeing tour by bus and then to a professional soccer game. Benjamin had never seen a professional soccer game. He had played as a child, but here he was at a professional game in this huge stadium with people screaming.

They also brought in a Jewish professor who taught classes in Yiddish to the children at the youth hostel. Although the children came from different places, they developed friendships.

The trip to London was the first time Benjamin had been on a ship. It was a very rough voyage and Benjamin, along with most of the others, got sick. It was worth the price. When they arrived in London, they were taken to a youth hostel specifically designed for them. They were given pajamas. Benjamin had never seen pajamas. Benjamin had always slept in his underwear, as did all the adults. They were also given pocket money to buy cigarettes or candy. Benjamin was told that it was the British government that was providing everything and not a Jewish organization. However, the British did allow a Jewish organization to administer the program.

A day after he arrived in London Benjamin was asked if he wanted a kosher hostel. About twenty-five boys opted for the kosher hostel, and they were sent to a house set up as a kosher hostel. There was another kosher hostel set up for girls, about a half an hour's walk from the boys' hostel. They would visit each other, usually on Saturdays.

One of the girls was from Benjamin's hometown. Benjamin knew her father, and she knew Benjamin's father. They knew each other. She was about a year younger than Benjamin, but they knew each other from school.

England took in youngsters to save them. America did not. America took no children and did nothing for the Jewish immigrants during the Truman administration.

Benjamin was placed in a beautiful house at 75 New Highbury Park in London, in one of the Jewish neighborhoods so Benjamin could walk to shul for Shabbas. Benjamin could walk to shul and visit with families. Families would invite the Jewish children for an afternoon on a Saturday. Benjamin and the other Jewish children would sing songs. It was a very positive experience for Benjamin.

While in London Benjamin made a call to Benjamin's brother-in-law's brother. He was younger than Benjamin and had been in England during the war. Youngsters were evacuated from London during the bombing and taken to Scotland or Ireland. He survived and later married. Benjamin called him when he arrived in London and told him who he was. He came to see Benjamin immediately. His name was Ralph Mandelbaum. His parents also treated Benjamin very kindly. Benjamin visited with them many times during his three years in London. He invited Benjamin to come and have Shabbas with him. This meant that Benjamin stayed there from Friday evening until Saturday evening. Ralph lived with his parents-in-law, in a big house, quite a distance from the hostel in a completely different neighborhood of London.

CHAPTER 45

When Ralph came to see Benjamin in the hostel, he brought Benjamin a beautiful dark blue suit with stripes. It was quite a luxury for Benjamin, and it was in good condition. Benjamin spent Shabbas with Ralph and his family many times.

The English government was ready to provide for the Jewish refugees as long as it was necessary for them to establish themselves to be able to earn their own living, but the refugees were told that they could not go to school. School cost money, and it would be a while before one could earn his or her own living if one went to school. It was a blow for Benjamin because Benjamin was brought up to study. He missed school, and he needed to catch up. They said no to school.

They encouraged Benjamin to choose a trade, so he chose to be a diamond cutter. He did not know much about diamonds or diamond cutting but it sounded like a good trade. Benjamin thought he could make a good living as a diamond cutter. They could not find a person who was willing to train Benjamin as an apprentice in diamond cutting. Benjamin was able to find one on his own, and he did start cutting diamonds. He gradually learned how to cut diamonds. When Benjamin dropped a diamond, he sometimes had to spend the whole day looking for it. You could not leave it on the floor. If you did not find it, the owner might think that you stole it.

The man who trained Benjamin in diamond cutting was a Hungarian Jew in his mid 30's. His family name was Alt. He paid Benjamin minimum wages, which was 30 shillings or 1.5 pounds a week as an apprentice at the time. For Hanukkah, he gave Benjamin a five pound bonus. He did not make any money on Benjamin because Benjamin cut the diamonds too slowly. Benjamin wanted to cut the stones perfectly so he spent too much time on each stone. Benjamin would not even let a minor imperfection go. He had to work on it until it was perfect.

Mr. Alt decided because of Benjamin's perfectionism and Benjamin's good work habits to put Benjamin on another style of cutting where perfectionism was necessary, the finer cuts of diamonds. Benjamin was taken off rough cutting and was put on fine cutting, called "brillianting." Benjamin did very well. He still was not fast, but he made a nice stone.

Benjamin did that from 1946 through 1949, but he was not happy in England. In the beginning there was euphoria coming from hell to London, but it did not last long. It was not London's fault or the people who provided for Benjamin. It was Benjamin's fault. He was restless. He was being transplanted from one kind of life to a completely new life, a new language, a new culture. Everything was new and different. Benjamin did not take to it well. He did not have what is called in Yiddish, sitzfleisch. Sitzfleisch means the patience to sit down and stay seated. Benjamin was boiling, so he did all sorts of things that he later regretted. He worked at a grocery store for one of his relatives. He could not settle down, so he finally registered to go to America.

Benjamin's older brother was already in America. One of Benjamin's older sisters was already in America. Benjamin's older sister's husband had a brother in America for many years. He was one of the first to receive a visa to come to America after the war. He was able to come because of regulations that allowed immigration for close relatives. A brother was considered a close relative.

CHAPTER 46

Benjamin had been in England for more than a year when he registered with the American consulate to go to America. Most of the children wound up in America. A few went to Israel. In November 1949, Benjamin landed in Boston. In order to get to America Benjamin had to go to a displaced persons camp in Germany or Austria to be registered. Benjamin came to America from a displaced persons camp. He did not come from London because he could not get a visa from there. This camp was in Austria and was called Bialik. Bialik was a famous Hebrew poet and writer in the early part of the century in the '20s and '30s. Benjamin registered at Camp Bialik and in a few weeks he was on a ship to America. The trip took about eight or nine days. The name of the ship was the S.S. Muir.

Benjamin arrived in Boston in early November 1949 on a Friday. Since Benjamin was religious, he would not ride a train on the Sabbath. Benjamin and a number of others who were with him were placed with Jewish families for the Sabbath until they could take a train Saturday night to New York. Everybody went to New York.

The family Benjamin stayed with on the Sabbath was very nice to Benjamin to him. They spoke Yiddish as well as English at the table, not knowing that Benjamin understood both. Benjamin found it very humorous. The mother, father, and two daughters always spoke in Yiddish to Benjamin. They did not know that Benjamin understood every word of English. Benjamin had lived in England. Benjamin never told them he spoke English.

The family lived on Commonwealth Avenue about ten minutes from a shul. Benjamin stayed there just for the Sabbath. Saturday night he took a train to New York. Benjamin's brother was living in New York. While Benjamin was in England, his older sister, her husband, and Benjamin's brother had all immigrated to America in 1948. The younger of Benjamin's two older sisters was still in Europe.

Benjamin's older sister could not get to Palestine because it was illegal at the time. If you tried to immigrate to Palestine, you would wind up in Cyprus if the British intercepted your ship going to Palestine. There was a very big camp in Cyprus with barbed wires that reminded people of the concentration camps. That is where you would be kept if you were caught.

Benjamin had not seen his brother in three or four years. His brother had a nice room, and there was an extra bed for Benjamin. Benjamin roomed with his brother in the Williamsburg section of Brooklyn in a very Hasidic neighborhood. These were Benjamin's people. He felt warm among them, and he respected them, and he trusted them. Then Korea came.

It was early 1950, and the Korean War was starting up. America was drafting into its armies even people who came off the ship yesterday, if they came in as legal immigrants. In England you had to be a citizen to be drafted into their armies. In America, if you had a green card, you had to serve your country. Benjamin survived the concentration camps only to come to the United States to be sent over to Korea to die as a soldier. He did not think that was fair. If he lived here for five years and became a citizen, he would be obligated to his new country. But, he was here only for a few months, and he had to register for the draft.

He registered for the draft, but he also went to a private doctor in Brooklyn. The doctor examined Benjamin.

Benjamin asked the doctor, "Will they take me?"

The doctor said, "They will take you. You have no medical problems; no mental disease, no physical disease."

The doctor did not know about any mental diseases because he was not a psychiatrist. Benjamin had plenty of mental problems. A military psychiatrist would probably have rejected him.

But, Benjamin decided not to stay and wait to be drafted. If President Clinton could dodge the draft for Vietnam, a boy coming out of concentration camps could not be blamed for not wanting to go and die in a foreign country after a few months of residence in America.

CHAPTER 47

In New York Benjamin worked as a diamond cutter and saved a little money. New immigrants were provided for when they first arrived until they found employment. The Joint Distribution Committee, Joint for short, gave the new immigrants enough to pay for a room and for food. They insisted you find a job. They would not let you go to school. Benjamin had a woman social worker see him every week to see what progress he was making. Benjamin received twenty-five dollars a week, just enough to live on.

Benjamin lived with his brother, and they ate out in those delicatessen restaurants in New York. They were very inexpensive. They could not cook by themselves. They did not have a kitchen. Benjamin's older sister lived in Cleveland, Ohio.

When the social worker asked Benjamin what kind of job he wanted, Benjamin told her he had some experience with diamond cutting, and he would like to continue with that work.

The social worker, said, "No, I can't find you a job in diamond cutting."

After six weeks in New York she said, "I have a job for you."

Benjamin said, "What kind of job?"

She said, "A *gopher* to run from one office to another to deliver messages and mail. It pays $30 or $35 a week."

Benjamin said, "I don't want it."

Benjamin was taken off the list of receiving money from the government, and now he was on his own. Benjamin managed to find a place to work as a diamond cutter on his own. The business was located on 47th Street. The man in charge, Mr. Engel, was a Slovakian Jew. Benjamin made a little more every week because he kept getting better at diamond cutting.

Benjamin knew that if you were a student, you would get a student deferment, so he thought he could avoid Korea by going to yeshiva. The idea of going to Brazil came much later. First Benjamin became a student. The summer of 1950, Benjamin's first year in America, Benjamin left his diamond-cutting job and went to Atlantic City to work for the season. He did not get a job as a waiter. He got a job as a busboy. He had to carry heavy trays, some weighing twenty or thirty pounds, full of dishes, with food or without food. That was Benjamin's first job in the food industry. He worked in a luxurious resort hotel for a couple of weeks as a busboy. Then he found work in a small guesthouse, also known as a rooming house. There were many small homes where you could rent a room with food. Benjamin got a job from a Hungarian woman in Atlantic City for the whole summer. There were no busboys there. Benjamin graduated to become a waiter. He made a little money, but he had the best food.

When the season was over, Benjamin had to go back to New York. That is when Benjamin got in touch with this man from Brazil. Benjamin heard about him. The man was from Benjamin's hometown and was now living in Rio de Janeiro. He knew Benjamin's family.

He told Benjamin, "You can come here, and I'll help you get settled."

So Benjamin went to Rio de Janeiro, Brazil in January of 1951, barely a year after his arrival in the United States out of fear of being drafted.

Benjamin arrived in Rio de Janeiro and about a week later, Benjamin's contact had a job for Benjamin. Benjamin was told that the jobs available for Jews in Brazil where peddler jobs. There were many different things to peddle, but much of it was fabrics for clothing for women. They would carry these fabrics from door to door in the villages, and these would be sold on consignment.

Although the poor village women wanted nice quality fabric, they could not afford to pay for it. The way it worked was you would get a down payment that amounted to almost all of what was paid in wholesale for the item, and then you would collect the rest in small amounts over many months. If the person stopped making payments, there was nothing you could do. This was a lucrative business in South America. It was called "clapping." The peddler would come to a house and would announce his presence by clapping. Clapping, right outside the door, and that is how the peddler made his living. By the time Benjamin arrived in Brazil, some of these peddlers were already millionaires building apartment houses.

However, the job his friend had for Benjamin was as a Hebrew teacher in a resort outside of Rio de Janeiro. Although many people would go there for the summer, there were also a number of Jews living there permanently. They needed a Hebrew teacher.

Benjamin said, "I'm not a teacher, I never taught."

"Don't worry, you know enough for them, you know more than enough for them," he told Benjamin.

Benjamin job was to teach children how to read and write and speak Yiddish and a little Hebrew if necessary, but mostly Yiddish. These were Yiddish speaking families. All Eastern European Jews. Some were observant, most were not.

On a Sunday afternoon, Benjamin was taken to that town in the mountains to meet with the *machers,* the leaders of the community to be interviewed. They interviewed him and liked him.

Benjamin said, "I am not a teacher."

They said, "What you have to teach you know plenty. If our children will learn a fraction of what you know, that's plenty."

Benjamin was a yeshiva boy and Yiddish was Benjamin's mother tongue. Benjamin was hired on the spot with substantial wages. But Benjamin did not have a visa to work. Benjamin came with a transit visa only good for thirty days and not extendable. You could not get a visa to Brazil in those days unless you had a national passport, and Benjamin was traveling on a stateless travel document. Benjamin was told that he could get a regular tourist visa in Paraguay. So Benjamin went to Paraguay.

Benjamin was given a letter and sent to the Brazilian embassy in Asuncion, the capital of Paraguay. When Benjamin arrived at the Brazilian embassy with the letter, Benjamin was told that he could not obtain a tourist visa. Benjamin was now stuck in Paraguay. He did not want to go back to New York. He just fled from there.

As it turned out, Paraguay also needed a Jewish teacher. So Benjamin agreed to stay as a teacher in Paraguay. Benjamin was paid 2,000 Guaraní, which was a good wage. Benjamin taught three sections a day. In the morning he taught children how to write, read, and speak Yiddish. The children understood some Yiddish because their parents spoke some Yiddish, but they were not fluent. Among themselves, they spoke Spanish. Benjamin did not know a word of Spanish, so Benjamin was given a teacher to learn Spanish. They paid for a teacher, but the teacher did not know how to teach. She taught Benjamin grammar but not the language. Benjamin learned to speak Spanish from the children.

In the morning Benjamin had about fifteen elementary children to teach. In the afternoon, Benjamin had another twenty elementary children. The schools in Paraguay had half-day school programs. Some students went in the morning and some went in the afternoon. In the evening Benjamin had high school students, who had some Yiddish education in previous years. Benjamin taught Yiddish and some religious observances. Benjamin taught in a school building. There was also a separate synagogue with a large auditorium. After about a week in Paraguay, Benjamin was unsure whether he wanted to stay.

The anniversary of the Holocaust, a day established by Israel, was a date where all over the world is set aside for commemorating and mourning for the victims of the Holocaust. Benjamin was asked to speak on that day. Benjamin had never spoken in public. After a speech commemorating the victims you have to chant the El Malei Rachamim. You cannot say the El Malei Rachamim without chanting it, cantorial style. How could Benjamin say no? Benjamin was a survivor. There were other survivors, but Benjamin was their teacher.

Benjamin spoke about the victims, about the horrors, about the pain, the suffering that still goes on, and people cried like babies, men and women. A few of them were also survivors, but the older ones were not. Then Benjamin was to chant the El Malei Rachamim. Benjamin composed the music in his mind walking in the streets in Paraguay. Benjamin took the music from a cantorial that he knew and used it with new words. It was very successful. Everyone started calling Benjamin the teacher or Senior Sharnofsky. Benjamin was almost twenty-three. He decided to stay in Paraguay and teach.

Arrangements were made for Benjamin to have kosher food and eat with the old shochet. Benjamin rented a room by himself and stayed in Paraguay for about two and a half years. Benjamin picked up Spanish very easily. But Benjamin did not want to stay there. Benjamin had *shpilkes*.[21] Paraguay was not a civilized

---

[21] Nervous energy.

society. Benjamin took the job under duress. He had no choice. He was in trouble. Benjamin wanted to leave Paraguay after six months, but it took him two and half years because Benjamin had no passport and no citizenship.

CHAPTER 48

Benjamin finally bought an identity card, but he got caught. The man who sold it to Benjamin was put in prison and so was Benjamin. This bogus identity card cost Benjamin $500.00. They put Benjamin in detention at the police station, which was not so bad, but the community was enraged with Benjamin when they found out that he wanted to leave. They were so enraged they did not help him. If they wanted to, they could have gotten Benjamin out after two hours, but they left him there.

Benjamin heard one man on the school committee who hired Benjamin, say, "*zol er foyln* in prison, let him rot there."

Not everybody felt that way; there were some families who were sympathetic. Benjamin had a girlfriend at that time, one of Benjamin's own students, a high school girl, who was fifteen or sixteen years old. She made the first steps. Her father and mother tried to help him. Eventually, Benjamin got out with the help of a rich jeweler, a survivor, who had a friend in the military who then ruled the country.

Benjamin was in detention for about two months. And then for one week during those two months, in the middle of those two months, they put Benjamin in an actual jail with real prisoners, real criminals. It was almost worse than a concentration camp. The prisoners could kill you, rape you, or do whatever they wanted. There was no supervision inside the prison. The prison was locked in with no guards inside. The food they gave you was inedible. Benjamin's girlfriend's mother brought Benjamin food daily.

After a week of this, Benjamin's girlfriend's parents convinced one of the Jews in the town who had influence with some generals to at least take him out of jail, back to the police station rather than staying in jail.

After this episode, Benjamin was the pariah of the Jewish community because he left the school without a teacher. He could not get out of the country because he did not have the necessary papers so he was stuck there. He did manage to get two jobs, one as an outside salesperson travelling the countryside selling farm equipment for an American firm in Paraguay, and the other job selling custom jewelry. Benjamin needed to make enough money to buy the necessary papers to leave Paraguay. It took Benjamin a year and a half to save the money he needed. Benjamin did have a brother in New York who was working at the Needle Trade but had a family to support and could not help. Benjamin had a sister in England, but her husband did not make much money, she had a large family, and she could not help. There was only one person that could have helped Benjamin, his older sister in Cleveland, Ohio. She escaped the worst of the Holocaust. Benjamin needed about $300 or $400, but she refused to help.

Shortly after Benjamin's return to Rio de Janeiro, a cousin who then lived in the second largest city in Brazil, San Paulo, hearing of Benjamin's return to Rio, contacted him and told Benjamin he could get Benjamin a job at a well established Hebrew school. A year earlier Benjamin helped this cousin get a visa to Brazil. The cousin had been in Germany and could not immigrate to America.

When he heard that Benjamin was in Paraguay, he contacted Benjamin. He sent Benjamin $500, and Benjamin was able to mail him his papers, and his cousin came to Rio de Janeiro.

CHAPTER 49

After living in Paraguay for a total of two and half years, Benjamin found a person who worked in the justice system and for a considerable sum of money issued Benjamin a brand new identity stating that Benjamin was a naturalized citizen. This card was stamped and signed by the proper official.

Benjamin did not have a passport so he could not leave Paraguay by air but was able to take the little boat that daily crossed the river from Asunción to Encarnación, Argentina. The trip took only ten or fifteen minutes, but as Benjamin stepped onto Argentina soil, he felt elation similar to the way he felt when emancipated. From there he took a bus to Buenos Aries.

When he arrived in Buenos Aries, Benjamin went to the Jewish community where they found him a place to stay with a Hungarian family. After a couple of weeks, Benjamin then went to the chief rabbi of Argentina, Rabbi Blau—a Hungarian Jew who had spent some time in Israel. At home the Rabbi spoke only Hebrew with his children. The Rabbi saw to it that the agency in charge of helping out families in need gave Benjamin a ticket on a boat to Brazil. Benjamin returned to Brazil to take the job first offered to him in January 1951. Because the Brazilian embassy in Asuncion denied Benjamin the visa, he got stuck in Paraguay until the summer of 1954.

Benjamin went back to Rio de Janeiro and stayed with the same family that he stayed with two and a half years earlier. Benjamin was able to get a job working early in the morning with a shochet. The shochet went several times a week to the slaughterhouse to slaughter meat in the kosher way. You have to examine the liver and the lungs. After working with the shochet for three or four weeks, Benjamin's cousin living in San Paulo, Brazil, told Benjamin he had a job for Benjamin as a teacher in Sao Paulo. His father and Benjamin's mother were first cousins. Benjamin did not know this cousin before the war. He did know his mother who used to visit when Benjamin was still a child. Two of his younger brothers were in Melk with Benjamin, but

Benjamin did not know this until a couple of weeks before the evacuation from Melk.

Benjamin met his cousin's younger brother in Melk one day while marching up the hill to the camp after a night shift. Benjamin asked him where he was from, and he named the village Venif. Benjamin told him he had relatives there, the Ganz family. Then he told Benjamin that was his family. They were in a different block, and Benjamin had never seen them before that time. Benjamin would not have known them even if he had seen them or even worked with them in Melk

Benjamin went to San Pablo and moved in with his cousin. Benjamin's cousin was a single man, about four years older than Benjamin. He had a room and a family where he ate kosher food.

Benjamin was able to get a job teaching high school students who did not know Spanish. They knew only Portuguese, and some of them knew Yiddish. Benjamin taught until the school year ended, but he did not have a good chance of getting a job for the following year because there was surplus of Israelis that wanted to teach, and they all spoke Hebrew better than Benjamin. In January 1954 Benjamin decided to go back to the United States. Benjamin went by boat that took about fourteen days. He arrived in New York and found work as a diamond cutter in Manhattan. He was paid on a piecework basis.

What Benjamin really wanted to do was to go to Yeshiva University, but he had no money, no high school diploma, and no sponsor.

Although Yeshiva University had plenty of money, when Benjamin showed up, they told him they had no money for him. So Benjamin went to a man in New York Benjamin knew from Solotvyno. The man was a great scholar and a banker. He knew Benjamin's father very well and knew Benjamin because they were liberated together in the same camp, Gunskirchen, Austria. Benjamin met him in Mauthausen about a month before the end of the war. His name was Aaron Magid.

Aaron told Benjamin, "I'll go to Klein, the owner of the Barton Chocolates, and see if we can set you up."

Klein was a Hungarian Jew. Klein had given money to Yeshiva University, and he was able to get Benjamin accepted to Yeshiva University. Benjamin met with Rabbi Sachs at the

Yeshiva University to be tested. You had to be tested in order to be placed in the proper grade level.

Rabbi Sachs told Benjamin, "Pick out a page any place in the Talmud and come here next week, prepare yourself."

He wanted to see whether Benjamin could study Talmud. Benjamin came back after a week, and Rabbi Sachs asked Benjamin a few questions, which Benjamin could answer. Then he asked Benjamin a question Benjamin could not answer.

"Rabbi, what you're asking me, that subject appears three or four pages later, I am only prepared for the first page," Benjamin said.

Rabbi Sachs expected Benjamin to research the first subject of the first page and go further into the book and find relevant information. Rabbi Sachs told the principal of the high school in charge of admission that Benjamin studied Talmud "like the Hungarian Jews do, not the way we, the Litvaks do (Jews from Lithuania are called Litvaks)." Benjamin did not know there were two ways of studying Talmud, the Hungarian way, or any other way. As far as Benjamin was concerned Talmud was Talmud, and you studied until you knew it. Benjamin thought this was an outrageous thing for him to say.

No one told Benjamin if he was accepted to study, so he went back to the high school to speak to the principal, Rabbi Abrams to find out.

Rabbi Abrams told Benjamin, "Here is a paper, pencil, write an application in Hebrew that you want to be accepted and why you should be accepted and so forth, give a little biography of yourself."

Benjamin could write in Hebrew, and he gave Rabbi Abrams the written application. Rabbi was very impressed, but he told Benjamin, "the problem's going to be tuition, how are you going to pay for yourself?"

Benjamin said, "I don't have any money to pay for myself. I'd like you to give me a scholarship."

"Oh," he said, "We don't have scholarships."

Then Benjamin told him, "I'm going to work. I'll be a full-time student and a part-time worker. I know how to cut diamonds, and all I have to make is $25 or $30 a week to sustain myself at the school."

"We can't let you work and study because you will not be able to do both", he said.

"Then give me a scholarship", Benjamin asked.

Then, he said to Benjamin, "Where are your parents?"

Benjamin said, "My parents died in Auschwitz."

"So who's going to pay for you?" he asked.

That was the end of the interview. Who is going to pay for you since your parents died in Auschwitz? You have no options. He showed Benjamin the door.

CHAPTER 50

When Benjamin returned to New York in 1954, he did not go back to Yeshiva University, he went to the Jewish Theological Seminary, and they accepted him with open arms. They did not quibble about tuition. They gave Benjamin a test and put him in the second year of the Teacher's Institute, a four-year program plus a fifth year part-time. A couple of weeks in the second year class the teachers told Benjamin he should skip the second and third years and go directly into the fourth year. There was one teacher who was against it because Benjamin's Hebrew was not fluent, so they decided to place him into the third year.

The seminary had a placement office where they provided Benjamin a part-time job in Nutley, New Jersey, in a private home teaching six students. The parents were not satisfied with the quality of Jewish education their children were receiving. Benjamin was making about $30 a week. The parents knew that was not enough to live on and convinced a Newark Rabbi that if they hired Benjamin to teach at their Hebrew school, they would all join the synagogue. That is how Benjamin got his first teaching job in America, teaching in Newark, New Jersey.

He graduated from the Jewish Theological Seminary in 1957 and received a scholarship to study in Israel at the Chaim Greenberg School designed for teachers who would be teaching in countries other than Israel. Unfortunately, Benjamin's Paraguayan passport had expired, and he was detained in France. Benjamin was told that for $500 his passport could be renewed. Benjamin had no money. He had a ticket to go to Israel and a ticket to go back to New York. So Benjamin was stuck in Paris for three months until his brother sent him money to travel back to New York. The program in Israel had started, and Benjamin was in no mood to go. He lived day to day in Paris with help from the Jewish community.

When Benjamin finally returned to America, there were no teaching jobs, so he went to Miami to work as a busboy. While a student at the seminary, Benjamin had worked as a busboy at

Grossinger's during Passover. Benjamin was able to get a job at the Waldman Hotel, a kosher restaurant in Miami Beach. After Passover there was no more work in Miami Beach, so he traveled by car with another man to Seattle, Washington and from there took a plane to Anchorage, Alaska to work as a waiter. Alaska had just become a state in 1958 and was paying very high wages. Benjamin was given room and board. He saved all his money because he wanted to leave Alaska before the winter.

Benjamin met a Jewish chaplain on the Air Force base there who supplied Benjamin with Kosher food. Before winter came Benjamin moved to San Francisco where he met a boyhood friend from Solotvyno who was teaching at a Hebrew school. He was able to help Benjamin get a job teaching there. The following year Benjamin was able to get a job as a principal at a Hebrew school in Oakland. Benjamin stayed there for two years and then moved to Los Angeles to teach in 1960.

Benjamin had a first cousin on his father's side who lived in Los Angeles. He was Benjamin's only cousin who survived the war. He had a small importing business in Los Angeles, but did not make very much money. His wife was also from Solotvyno. She was the only one in her family who survived the war.

In the summer of 1962 Benjamin was invited to attend his nephew Morris's bar mitzvah in Philadelphia. Benjamin's sister invited all her living relatives. This was a big change in Benjamin's life. Benjamin went to Philadelphia and helped prepare Morris for his bar mitzvah.

While in Philadelphia, Benjamin visited the Park Synagogue where he was offered a job as assistant principal. $8,000 a year was quite respectable too. At the time, it was the largest conservative temple in the country. Benjamin mostly taught but also conducted Shabbat services for students and conducted Seders for Passover.

While Benjamin was living in Los Angeles, he met Jean, a young lady from Argentina. Although she returned to Argentina, she continued to correspond with Benjamin. Benjamin's brother-in-law was able to arrange a permanent visa for Jean to come to Philadelphia as a housekeeper to join Benjamin so they could get married. Benjamin went to New York to find a better job. He left Jean with his sister. Benjamin was able to find a job in

Queens. Benjamin and Jean were married on August 5, 1963, packed up their car and moved to New York.

Benjamin began work at his new job and went back to school to complete his bachelor's degree at Columbia University. Jean was able to get a teaching fellowship at Queens College teaching Spanish and was paid $2,000 for the year.

Jean stayed in Benjamin's sister's house for a few days. Benjamin had an uncle who survived the war, Benjamin's mother's brother. He survived and three of his children survived, two boys and a girl. Benjamin did not meet these cousins until after the war. They lived in Toronto, Canada. His uncle was very wealthy. When he heard that Benjamin was getting married, he sent $200 to Benjamin's sister to give to Benjamin as a wedding gift. Benjamin met one of his sons at the Bar Mitzvah. Benjamin needed the money badly to pay for the wedding as small as it was. Instead of giving the money to Benjamin, his sister took the money and said it was to pay for rent when they lived in his sister's house because Benjamin did not pay enough while they lived in the house. When Benjamin found out, he called his uncle. His uncle was outraged.

CHAPTER 51

His sister's family was supposed to visit the uncle that summer, but when the uncle learned what his sister did, the uncle called it off.

The uncle said, "I don't care how much he owes you, you can't take away the wedding gift."

His sister still refused to give Benjamin the $200 wedding gift, so his uncle sent Benjamin another $200. His uncle told his sons that they should also send Benjamin a wedding gift, but Benjamin's sister told them not to. Because of his sister's interference, Benjamin's brother and sister did not come to Benjamin's wedding. Benjamin had a sister in town, a brother in New York, and a sister in Philadelphia and none of them showed up.

Benjamin had some friends, who came to the wedding, from Solotvyno, people he knew since childhood, and some friends they made during their stay in Cleveland. Benjamin was miserable. You are supposed to be happy when you get married, but not Benjamin. Other families cross oceans to attend weddings. People come from Europe, from Israel, from California. It was very, very painful.

Benjamin and Jean were married in the famous Park Synagogue, one of the largest synagogues in the country, and the next day they left for New York and their life together. Benjamin spent several hundred dollars on the dinner. He received one present from a Solotvyno lady who sent a set of towels, and one other present from Isaac who was with Benjamin in the camps. Isaac lived a few miles outside of Cleveland. Isaac came to Cleveland and told Benjamin that he could not come to the wedding because of a previous commitment. He gave Benjamin a $25 check. Under normal circumstances Benjamin would not have accepted this from a friend like him, but Benjamin was broke.

August 4, 1963, was a very dark day for Benjamin. Getting married is supposed to be wonderful, a holiday, a big event in one's life. You start a new life with a mate. Benjamin was darkened because his only surviving brother and sisters, although close by chose not to come. Benjamin did get a few telegrams, one from a cousin in Los Angeles, and one from a teacher in California.

The next day Benjamin and Jean packed everything they owned in their 1956 Buick and went to New York. Benjamin showed up at the synagogue in New York with no place to live. He met with the rabbi, and the rabbi's secretary said she would take them in. She had a basement apartment, and they could live there until they found their own apartment.

After a year in New York, Benjamin left to teach in Cranford, New Jersey for an annual salary of $7,500. The next year he became principal and held the position for four years. During this time Benjamin was also taking courses at New York University. When he left Columbia University in 1964, Benjamin received two degrees, one from Columbia University and one from the Jewish Theological Seminary.

After leaving Columbia University, Benjamin continued his studies at Hunter College where his tuition was free for students training to be teachers, but because he did not like the professors there he transferred to New York University and received a Master's Degree in education from New York University in 1967.

Benjamin's wife Jean had finished a two-year program at Queens College for her Master's Degree in education. Jean had received her B.A. in education at New York University. After she received her Master's Degree, she immediately went back to New York University for postgraduate courses and obtained her 60 credits needed for a Ph.D. degree. Although she met all the requirements for her Ph.D. she did not write a thesis, because she became pregnant, and Benjamin and Jean travelled to Israel with an American passport.

The trip to Israel came about through a guest lecturer, Dr. Kutcher, a professor from Hebrew University in Jerusalem. Dr. Kutcher took a liking to Benjamin and offered Benjamin and his wife Jean full scholarships to do post graduate work at Hebrew University in Jerusalem. It was an offer that Benjamin could not pass up. So they packed their bags and off they went to Israel in 1967.

While they were taking courses at Hebrew University, their daughter Sarah was born on October 28 at the world-renowned Hadassah Hospital in Jerusalem.

They returned to the United States in 1969, and Benjamin took a teaching position in Pittsburgh. Then in 1973, when his contract was not renewed, Benjamin came to Lexington, Massachusetts. The placement office of the Jewish Theological seminary in New York found Benjamin the position in Lexington as the principal of a Hebrew school. It was his experience in Lexington that convinced Benjamin that he would never seek another job in the Hebrew schools.

The Rabbi was serving as the principal of the Hebrew school in 1973 when Benjamin arrived, and the year before a woman served in that capacity. She was paid very little. Benjamin insisted that he be paid an annual salary of $18,000 the first year and $19,000 the second year based on his experience and background. The entire congregation interviewed Benjamin because the only way there would be money to pay Benjamin was to raise the membership fees.

The congregation appointed a committee, and they held regular monthly meetings with Benjamin. A woman, who studied Hebrew and knew Hebrew from Hebrew College in Boston, was put in charge of the committee. From Benjamin's perspective, this was a big mistake. She thought she knew everything better than Benjamin. Benjamin made a presentation at one meeting in the winter of 1973 explaining what he intended to do as principal.

After the presentation a woman who was knitting raised her hand and said, "Mr. Sharnofsky, I don't think it's a good idea."

That killed it. Nobody discussed it, not even the rabbi who should have supported Benjamin. Despite all of this, the congregation agreed to hire Benjamin as principal for the Hebrew school at an annual salary of $18,000.

Benjamin was so discouraged with the situation that he told them he would not be seeking reappointment. Furthermore, Benjamin decided that he would never again teach at a temple or religious school. Between 1974 and 1976, Benjamin sold life insurance for Metropolitan Life.

CHAPTER 52

Benjamin was certified to teach Hebrew, Spanish, Social Studies, and History. Benjamin had a Master's Degree plus fifteen, and twenty-five years of teaching experience. This placed Benjamin at the highest level for salary for a public school teacher, and it made it very difficult to find work teaching in a public school.

Finally, Benjamin found a teaching position at a public school in Linwood. The High School was looking for a Hebrew teacher, and Benjamin applied, along with several others. Benjamin was selected to teach Hebrew in the language department. There was no comparison in experience or education between Benjamin and the other candidates.

Benjamin kept having this recurring nightmare. He dreamt that he was deported from New York. He was being forced to march with a large mass of people. They were guarded on both sides. It was already late afternoon, it became evening, and still they were marching. The guards were wearing civilian uniforms, but he knew that they were being taken to Auschwitz. Benjamin is marching, and a friend of Benjamin, a tall man, an American friend living in Madrid, Spain, was marching with him. And Benjamin kept thinking, "God, I will not survive this time around, how could I?"

Then all of a sudden Benjamin's friend disappears. His friend was carrying a heavy load. Benjamin did not know whether he disappeared because he stayed behind and could not walk fast enough, or he was still in the transport, or that he escaped. Benjamin was frantic. They came to a place where people were drinking water. He saw no guards. He walked away. There was a road. Benjamin was walking. There was an old man walking to a house. Benjamin walked behind him.

Benjamin said to the old man, "I don't belong to that group."

Benjamin continued to walk behind the old man. They came to a yard with many leaves down. It was fall. It was not dark now. Benjamin decided to lie down. He thought if he kept walking, he would get lost. But if he lay down, maybe nobody would notice him at night. Then he heard them marching right by him.

"Mach schnell! Mach schnell!" The Germans would always tell you to go fast.

Benjamin lay there for a long time to make sure that the transport had left. Benjamin finally got up and tried to find a place to sleep. He sees another yard. It is a big yard with an old building. It could have been a church, or it could have been a synagogue. There were several people in the yard. He could not figure out what language they were speaking. Maybe they were speaking Yiddish.

Benjamin comes closer to the gate and through the wire gate, Benjamin cried, "*Ich bin a yid!* Let me in, I am a Jew, let me in!"

They let him in. No one talks to him. He sits there with the other people. Benjamin is still looking for a place to sleep. Finally, he gets up and goes into the house to find a place to sleep. There are two women inside. Benjamin has a few coins. He offers them half his money if they will let him sleep on the floor. They agree. There were also children in the house. Benjamin slept that night and escaped from the Germans.

Benjamin is constantly bombarded with these nightmares. In another nightmare he is watching a house burn.

Benjamin did not transplant very well after the war. He was best suited to his life in Solotvyno. He did the best he could under the circumstances.

"The jury has reached a verdict," shouted the court officer. Benjamin was jolted out of his past nightmares to the present.

"Are all counsel present in the courtroom?" asked the judge.

"We are your honor," said both attorneys.

Looking at the court officer, the judge said, "Bring the jurors in."

Eighteen minutes later the twelve jurors walked into the courtroom.

"The court is in session. Please rise for the Court," intoned the courtroom clerk.

After the judge sat down, the courtroom clerk stated, "You may be seated. The court is in session in the case of Sharnofsky verses Linwood School Committee."

The judge looking directly at the foreperson of the jury inquired, "Has the jury reached a verdict?"

The foreperson looking back at the judge said, "Yes we have your honor."

The judge said, "Please hand your verdict slip to the court officer," as the court officer reached for the verdict slip being handed to him by the foreperson.

While the judge was looking at the verdict slip, Sarah was holding Benjamin's hand. Benjamin was pale. He felt numb.

The judge read the verdict slip, "We find in favor of the defendant Linwood School Committee that they committed no religious or age discrimination against the plaintiff Benjamin Sharnofsky."

As Benjamin fainted, God looked down and wept.

EPILOGUE

"Those who cannot remember the past are condemned to repeat it."
George Santayana

Benjamin accepted his fate. After all he is a Jew. Jews are destined to suffer. Benjamin believed that he survived for a reason - to tell his story so that no one would ever forget. Benjamin began his new career, going from school to school, telling the students about the holocaust as only a survivor could.

He asked me to write his story for those who did not survive, for the children, for the children's children, and all the children to come.

Benjamin taught me that even out of this hell of hells some good came – The birth of Israel, the one and only Jewish state, where Jews could come from anywhere and gain entry and citizenship. But at what a price! Why did the civilized countries turn their backs on the Jews and let them be slaughtered?

Few survived the ordeal. Even in this hell of hells, Benjamin said you had a choice to hope, to struggle, to survive. The Germans could torture you, rape you, starve you, and kill you. While their treatment was inhumane, the Germans could not take away your humanity, your hope, or your will to survive.